MURDER IN THE GARDEN

When I looked up, I saw that Bardot was embracing her green paw and had been working feverishly on the far corner of the plot.

I need to nip this in the bud.

"Bardot, no more." She looked at me with a big grin on her muddy face, and promptly went back to digging. I figured "just this once" and secured all the contents of my find back into the cigar tin.

I heard Bardot give off a high-pitched whine and noted that her digging had stopped. She was crouching and backing away from the hole.

Then I spotted it, a still partially fleshy, liver-spotted hand that seemed to be reaching out from the grave. . . .

Books by Christine E. Blum

FULL BODIED MURDER

MURDER MOST FERMENTED

Published by Kensington Publishing Corporation

KENSINGTON BOOKS are published by

Kensington Publishing Corp.
119 West 40th Street
New York, NY 10018

All Kensington titles, imprints, and distributed lines are available at special quantity discounts for bulk purchases for sales promotion, premiums, fund-raising, educational, or institutional use. Special book excerpts or customized printings can also be created to fit specific needs. For details, write or phone the office of the Kensington Sales Manager: Kensington Publishing Corp., 119 West 40th Street, New York, NY 10018. Attn. Sales Department. Phone: 1-800-221-2647.

Kensington and the K logo Reg. U.S. Pat. & TM Off.

eISBN-13: 978-1-4967-1213-4
eISBN-10: 1-4967-1213-7
Kensington Electronic Edition: May 2018

ISBN-13: 978-1-4967-1212-7
ISBN-10: 1-4967-1212-9
First Kensington Mass Market Edition: May 2018

10 9 8 7 6 5 4 3 2 1

Printed in the United States of America

Murder
Most
Fermented

CHRISTINE E. BLUM

KENSINGTON PUBLISHING CORP.
www.kensingtonbooks.com

For all the ladies of the Rose Avenue Wine Club

Chapter 1

"DIRT?"

I said to my yellow Lab, Bardot, while we were trudging up the hill.

"For my birthday they got me dirt??"

As the incline sharpened, so did the weight of the wagon I was pulling behind me loaded with shovels and claws and other garden accoutrements that had been included with this, oh so thoughtful, gift.

Nothing about this early morning trip was pleasant until I had an idea. Slowly and without her noticing, I tied the end of Bardot's leash to the handle of the wagon. She couldn't have cared less because the promise of open space and critters filled her with excitement from her nose to her caudal vertebrae.

I prepared myself and took in some deep breaths from my diaphragm.

"SQUIRREL!" I yelled and then lowered myself

into the wagon like a Luge racer starting down the track.

We reached the top in no time, but here was the problem, Bardot hadn't found the squirrel yet. Which meant that we kept on going. She veered right and ran to the only thing better than a squirrel, people. To her excitement, she'd found not just adults but a team of four- and five-year-old Little Leaguers. When she stopped to be adored, I had two choices: do nothing and be convicted of manslaughter or do a self-imposed wipeout to stop the momentum of the wagon. I chose the latter and was dumped out onto the dirt road. A bright yellow kneeling pad with a smiling frog on it landed appropriately across my face. The group, assured that I was okay when I sat up, quickly went back to the Bardot lovefest.

Oh, she's working it all right.

This might be a good point to stop and bring you up to speed.

I am Halsey, which is actually a truncated moniker for Annie Elizabeth Hall, the name on my birth certificate. You can see why I needed a nickname shortly after being weaned. My parents were not playing some kind of cruel joke on me. They just weren't big Woody Allen fans. After that, they did a pretty good job of raising me.

I have my own company writing code and designing websites, a job that allowed me to pack up my toys and move to a Los Angeles beach community after my marriage and life in New York City went up in smoke. That was just over a year ago, and boy, have things changed.

You've met Bardot, she's an American Field Lab versus an English Lab; she's smaller, much leaner, and built with a Ferrari engine. She is hardwired to run through caustically thorny brambles and crash into pond ice to retrieve whatever form of fowl you have shot out of the sky. Since I am not a hunter, and the only ice that can be found three miles from the beach is crushed in a margarita, she has developed other skills. The highlight? She can dive underwater. Deep underwater. Try twelve feet underwater. Which actually saved my life once.

Now to the "they," I refer to the ones who celebrated the anniversary of my birth with a gift of dirt. I am proud to be part of this coterie of oenophiles who call themselves the "Rose Avenue Wine Club," because well, we all live on Rose Avenue and we all enjoy a touch of the grape. Our members range in age from thirty-two to eighty-seven and are an all-female cast of characters that imbibe shamelessly and say whatever comes to mind. Everyone has a story, and last year the group created a new one through crime and murder that now binds us together for life.

More on that later.

I'm not really being fair when I call my gift "dirt." I don't want to appear ungrateful, it really was very thoughtful on many levels and ties me more deeply to my new life in Mar Vista, California.

At the top and east side of Rose Avenue sits a hill that in the 1930s and '40s was home to truck farms producing vegetables to take to market. A particularly rich area for agriculture, Mar Vista historically played host to fields and fields of lima beans giving rise to the title, "Lima Bean Belt of the Nation."

The open land is still preserved today despite continuous offers from drooling developers and is home to a local Little League and a community garden offering six acres of fifteen-by-fifteen-foot plots of incredibly rich soil that seems to defy even the least adept of horticulturists.

My gift is making more and more sense.

I am told that, like any apartment in New York that has running water, people wait for the owners of these plots to die in order to pounce on the coveted patches of soil. That makes my share, which was not the result of a recent death but the final settlement of a probate, all the more special.

When it was time for the young boys of summer to take to the field and when most of the gardeners had dispersed, I righted my wagon, gathered the last modicum of dignity I possessed, and consulted my map for the plot's location. I had skinned knees and elbows, making this thirty-something look more like an overgrown middle grader.

The shade provided welcome relief as I plopped down beside my garden to be. I was pleasantly surprised to find that the soil had been turned over. With the drought, I had fully expected to see a dry crust from a long time of neglect. I wasn't planning to accomplish much today, this was basically a scouting mission to give me enough to do some substantive online research. You see, my plan was to grow grapes.

"Someday this will all be 'Halsey Vineyards,' Bardot."

She looked around wondering if any of the words in that sentence were euphemisms for "critter." My chore for the day was to start to aerate the soil to get it ready to accept and nurture the vines. This wasn't going to happen overnight, but at least I'd feel like I'd accomplished *something*.

I chose the shovel with the more tapered head and went to work. The goal was to loosen as much of the old soil as possible. Grapevine root systems like to run deep. This got Bardot curious; she'd never seen me do this kind of activity before. With each toss of the dirt, she peered into the hole, hoping for anything that moved.

Sure enough, after working a section for a bit, I hit something more than dirt. Something that made a clanging sound when the shovel made contact with it.

Great, I've probably hit a main pipe and killed the water for the entire hill.

I looked around to see if anyone could offer guidance, but I was alone. I dropped the shovel and bent down for a closer look. As I cleared a square of soil around the object, I was able to determine that it was a rusted metal box. With a little more digging and some help from Bardot, I managed to loosen it enough to get my fingers underneath and lift it to the surface. It had been painted red at one time, and after tilting it toward and away from the sun, I was able to make out writing that said LA UNION CIGARS.

Cool. I have just the spot for this antique in my office.
When I placed it in the wagon, I could feel something inside shifting. Once again I looked around, this time hoping that nobody was in viewing distance.

I used a small knife and delicately worked on the seal between the lid and the main box. It looked very old and may be worth something, so I didn't want to damage the box any more if I could help it. Like wrestling with opening a pickle jar, I finally heard the sound of air escaping and the lid popped up.

Inside I saw a piece of blue velvet fabric cut to fit snugly in the box. I carefully lifted it and placed it on the wagon. Beneath was a yellowed folded document. It had printed type on it as well as pen and ink handwriting. It all looked very official. When I opened it, I saw the words "DEED" and below the name "Anderson Rose" and the date "April 16, 1902."

I didn't want to risk exposing it to the elements, so I folded it back up and returned it to the box, facedown. On the back was written "Transfer of mineral rights." I hadn't a clue what all this meant, but my heart was racing. As I moved the box, I once again felt the weight of contents moving. It clearly wasn't coming from that light piece of paper. I noticed that the deed and the fabric only took up a small portion of the depth of the box, so there was something under the bottom piece of velvet. Carefully, I lifted the deed up, sandwiched between the two protective pieces of fabric. Underneath was what looked like a men's gold signet pinky ring, and it bore a strange-looking engraved crest and embellishment.

Cool.

When I looked up, I saw that Bardot was embracing her green paw and had been working feverishly on the far corner of the plot.

I need to nip this in the bud.

"Bardot, no more." She looked at me with a big grin on her muddy face, and promptly went back to digging. I figured "just this once" and secured all the contents of my find back into the cigar tin. I had a fun project, now dirt *is* good.

I heard Bardot give off a high-pitched whine and noted that her digging had stopped. She was crouching and backing away from the hole.

Then I spotted it, a still partially fleshy, liver-spotted hand that seemed to be reaching out from the grave.

Crap. Here we go again.

I had no choice but to call Detective Augie, the officer assigned to Mar Vista and someone I know well enough to have on speed dial. And not because we have some sort of civilian/civil servant romance going on. See, when I first moved to Rose Avenue I made an honest mistake and walked into the wrong house for my first Wine Club. How was I to know that there was a dead body in the backyard? It took a lot of work and convincing but ultimately the Wine Club girls and I were not only able to provide enough evidence to Augie to move me off the suspect list, but we also solved the murder. Surely lightning won't strike twice?

Bardot and I waited on the wagon at the top of the hill until the cops arrived. I had pleaded with Augie not to use the sirens, but I guess a couple of overzealous uniforms hadn't gotten the memo. I'll be retelling this story all day to the people on Rose Avenue.

One good thing about announcing their arrival is that I had a moment to think and decided that I'd keep the cigar box and its contents to myself a little longer to do some research. What would it hurt? I'm pretty sure that the two are not connected. . . .

When Augie returned from inspecting my plot and the body, he came over to me and sat down on a tree stump by my wagon.

"Halsey, Halsey, Halsey. What is it about you that attracts death and murderers? This was such a quiet community before you moved in."

"What? I'm a model citizen; besides I didn't discover the body, Bardot did. She's the one you need to talk to; I'm just an innocent bystander."

With that, Bardot relaxed her ears, gently walked over to Augie, licked his hand, and then sat down and gave him her most loving cocked head smile.

I have got to start taking her to auditions.

"This is not a joke, Halsey," Augie said while having trouble pulling his eyes away from Bardot's face. "This body is old but it didn't bury itself. And once again you are the one found at the scene. I'll do what I can, but don't be surprised if I have to bring you in for a talk. I already know that I'll get pressure from above."

"That's ridiculous. You can't blame me for this! Heck, this is my first time here! If I'd buried a body, then why on earth would I go and dig it up and tell you what I'd found?"

I could tell by the look on his face that my logic had struck a nerve.

"Perhaps, but this is how police procedure works. You can go for now, but stay close to home, we'll definitely need a follow-up with you. And take your dog, why does she keep staring at me?"

"She looooves you, Augie, she loooooooves you. Must be because you are so sweet."

"Go, get out of here."

I pulled Bardot on the wagon as we went down the hill while humming the k-i-s-s-i-n-g song.

Chapter 2

When we returned to my house, wagon with mystery cigar box in tow, I saw my neighbor Marisol staring out from my front stoop.

"Brought you your paper." She grinned, her back gold tooth catching the morning sunlight.

It was early even for her and she was still in her bathrobe, a flannel number with faded miniature roses and snaps for buttons. And fuzzy ankle socks and garden clogs. If I didn't know better, I'd guess that she was still waiting for a callback from her audition for *One Flew Over the Cuckoo's Nest*.

"You leave my paper up at the door every morning, Marisol. What makes today so special that I'm also graced with your presence in all your sartorial splendor?"

I say things like this just to mess with her. Marisol and I have a love/hate relationship. Meaning she loves to spy on me and I hate it. At eighty-something, I expect her to spend her days sitting in a recliner looking at photos of the old country,

Mexico, and watching telenovelas. But she eschews her heritage and wants to be seen as the all-American girl. With her jet-black dyed hair held back in combs and her landing strip of gray roots.

Truth be told, she saved my life once, and I may have saved hers. There is a love there that runs deep, but no form of torture would make me admit it.

"What are you gawking at? Can't you spy on the neighborhood from your own porch?"

"Shhh," she hissed.

I tower over Marisol at five eight, so I looked over her head and tried to follow her gaze. Despite the earlier wipeout, my hair still had the silky body that comes from almost annihilating it with highlighting chemicals, but I was blond again. And at thirty-five still in the game. Even if a certain bearded man was trying to take me off the market. But we get ahead of ourselves.

"That's what you're staring at, that lady walking her dog? What has she done to get a wild hair up your ass? Look, she's even picking up her dog's poop."

"Give it a minute. Whatcha got in that wagon? Did I hear sirens?"

I ignored her question and watched while the woman bagged the excrement, tied the package in a nice knot, and continued on her way. Just like we all do, having planned our route so our dogs do their constitutional as close as possible to a house where the trash bins are stored in front.

"This is ridiculous. I'm going in."

"Wait for it. Aha!"

The woman, unaware of her audience, stopped in front of house a few doors up, quietly opened the door of the iron mailbox, and dropped the bag inside. She then smiled and went on her way.

"Whoa," I said.

"She and Hawaii used to date. It didn't end well," Marisol explained.

"Hawaii" was her name for the divorced man who now lived by himself and always sported tropical print loose shirts. Underneath hung an ever-increasing belly.

"How long has this been going on?"

"Couple of weeks now; you should see what he does to her," Marisol replied, stepping down from my stoop.

"How do you always know these things??"

She was gone. One of Marisol's trademarks was her ability to vanish into thin air.

"Morning!" Sally greeted me while checking her step counter and breathing from her diaphragm. "Beautiful day like this makes me happier than a New York rat with a stuffed-crust pizza."

If I hadn't lingered another minute, I could have snuck inside the back gate under the radar. I was not ready to face my public yet, I wanted to shower and spend some time revisiting my newly found treasure.

"Hi, I was just getting my paper—"

Behind Sally approached two more Rose Avenue denizens.

"She's got me speed walking, says it's great exercise first thing in the morning. I can think of a far more pleasurable way to work out, and it doesn't involve getting out of bed."

"Tom," Aimee shrieked, giving her boyfriend's arm a love punch. They were festooned with so much digital gadgetry that it was a wonder they could walk at all.

"Glad to see you both," said Sally. "I'm doing Wine Club this afternoon. To celebrate the start of summer I'm pouring icy cold Crossbarn Rosé of Pinot Noir."

"Can I come?" Tom asked.

"NO," all three of us said in unison.

We were punctuated by a car horn and looked to the street where Penelope had stopped.

"Hello, luvs, what's up?" she asked in her cheery English accent.

"Wine Club at Sally's, four o'clock," we all shouted again.

The cars were backing up behind Penelope.

"See you then. Halsey, what on earth have you done to your knees?"

I was about to make up a story when a gentle tap of a car horn behind her sent Penelope waving and driving off.

"There's Peggy," Sally said, looking down the sidewalk across the street. "I'm going to remind her that she's bringing her crab-stuffed deviled eggs this afternoon."

Geez, I'm going to need a nap.

I shut the door, hoping that Bardot and I would finally get some peace and quiet at home in our little slice of paradise. I walked through the "great room" that spans the entire length of the house and includes a large dining and living room area, and went out the back French doors to retrieve my wagon. It was sitting where I'd left it on the other side of the gate.

One of the reasons I bought this house was that the garage had been converted to a small living space that, because I'm on a corner, can also be accessed from a door facing the side street. Which made it a perfect place for my office because it afforded me the ability to have distance between my work and personal life. Just outside the office and in the middle of my backyard is the pool, where Bardot the Diving Dog was born. Here's briefly how that came about: the day I moved into the house I was concerned that Bardot, still a puppy, would freak out if she fell into the pool. While at Whole Foods picking up some amazing produce, I saw a card from a guy touting his dog training skills. I called the number and he came by that afternoon. Jack, that's his name, had just barely stepped into the pool when Bardot jumped in after him, spun around in wild swimming circles, and shimmied up out from the side of the pool, thinking that this was indeed the life.

A bit later Jack wanted to do some laps and tossed me his watch to make swimming easier. Of course I missed it and the heavy timekeeper sank in the deepest end of the pool. SPLASH! All I could make out was the tip of a yellow tail disappearing under the surface. Moments later Bardot emerged with her quarry and proudly ran up the steps of the pool to examine her prize. Needless to say, Jack and I were gaping like lizards basking in the hot sun. Bardot was soon thinking that she was "all that and a bag of chips" and has worked diving into all sorts of situations. Including once diving into a public fountain to retrieve the coins.

We're not great in public.

I headed to the office while Bardot did a swan dive into the pool. I grabbed a Vitamin Water out of the mini fridge and took a refreshing gulp. Not wanting to waste any time preparing breakfast, I grabbed a jar of almond butter and a handful of peeled carrots and sat down at my desk. The first thing I did was to photograph the box from all sides as well as the contents. I carefully removed the document, afraid that from its old age anything could cause it to tear or just disintegrate. I wanted to handle it as little as possible, so I took a photo of both sides and then returned it to the velvet fabric. I placed both between two pieces of mailing cardboard and then stored it flat in a padded envelope. I may have gone a little overboard, but this was a deed and I could be coming into oil.

I may have to change my name to Elly May Clampett. . . .

With my desk lamp, I could get a much better view of the ring lying on the bottom layer of the box. If the dates are correct on the deed, then this ring could be over one hundred years old and very valuable. This needed to be handled with delicate care, but I wanted to get a better look at the ring. I could barely make out the engraved symbols on the sides, and I wondered if a name was also engraved somewhere. I grabbed the long-nose tweezers that I use to extract that tiny shred of paper that prevents the printer to function and grabbed the antique magnifying glass I'd pilfered from my dad's office as a kid to burn bugs in the summer.

I was just about to start my examination when the street door to my office opened.

"Hey, honey," Jack said. "What you got there?"

I looked at the six four man with his shaved head and nicely trimmed beard that had walked in. He was dressed for dog training in long shorts, hiking boots, and a pocketed belt that held treats, various kinds of collars, and the necessary blue doggie bags. He looked cute and despite a rocky start, I was happy to have him as my boyfriend. I call him my amber-eyed redwood.

Bardot, hearing her second-best friend, came running in soaking wet and slid into me on the wood floors, looking like a cartoon cow on ice. Jack snapped his fingers once and Bardot awkwardly righted herself and sat at attention. The ring went flying and the magnifying glass had fallen to the floor and cracked.

Oh crap, now I'm cursed for sure.

"Wow, that's some story. Remind me how these things always happen to you?" Jack asked after hearing about my dead body discovery and the procurement of the artifacts I'd been studying.

"Why I'm sure I don't know what you mean, Mr. Thornton," I said in my best Scarlett O'Hara accent. "I do declare, I was found innocent of all charges."

"You should probably talk to old Mr. Ott; he's a historian and chronicler of early California. Their house is like a museum. I'm headed over there this afternoon, I've been working with a pair of whippets they were given in exchange for an appraisal. Sweet dogs but pretty lively for a couple of seventy-year-olds."

"If I live that long, I have a feeling that this is much worse than breaking a ten-foot mirror." I sighed while on my hands and knees looking for the ring.

"It's a piece of glass, there's no bad luck in breaking that," he said, grinning and planting a kiss on my cheek. "See you Saturday; we'll have a wonderful dinner."

Bardot had remained statue still until the moment Jack left. She eyed me for a split second and then rolled on her back that she proceeded to scratch with serpentine wiggles. Leaving swirls of pool water in her wake.

I found the ring and looked at its inner side for any more clues. It was engraved with the Latin words "Memento Mori," a quick online search informed me that this means, "Remember you will die."

I just shouldn't have gotten out of bed this morning.

Chapter 3

"I hear it's going to be three stories," I heard Sally say as I walked onto her back patio for Wine Club. The usual suspects were there along with the newcomer that I'd heard about.

"I hope I won't be ruining your palates by contributing a couple bottles of Elgin Ridge Chardonnay, I thought that the summer fruit tastes would complement the Rosé," I said as I plopped down into Sally's last unoccupied wicker chair.

"There she is," said Peggy, "I hear that you're not a garden virgin anymore."

"Honey, the ship has sailed for anything that has 'Halsey' and 'virgin' in the same sentence," I said.

Peggy looks like everybody's favorite grandma. White-haired and fleeced in the winter, and hair under a baseball cap and madras sporting in the summer, she is someone you always want to hug. But as we learned last year, this sweet woman who is inching nearer and nearer to ninety has a past that included spying for the CIA. No, seriously, she did.

Sally decanted the wines and took a quick taste of each to make sure they were servable. At least that is how she's explained her actions in the past. Penelope helped distribute the filled glasses.

"I see you've cleaned up your knees, Halsey, but you still look like a girl who'd gotten into a row at the schoolyard."

"It's kind of a macabre story, which I'll get to after we've all imbibed a few fluid ounces," I replied, piquing everyone's interest.

Penelope is from England so we often find ourselves asking her to translate her indigenous words or phrases. In this case we'd already learned that "row" meant fight.

She'd moved to Rose Avenue late last year after accepting a sought-after curator position at a respected museum in town. Now the youngest in our group at twenty-eight, she brought both a degree of sophistication to the Wine Club along with a raucous appetite for fun and adventure.

"That looks sore," said Aimee, "want me to go get you some Bactine spray?"

"She's got some, it's in that glass she's holding," Peggy retorted in a jovial mood.

Aimee has gone through a lot of struggles in the year that I've known her, but it appears that she's close to coming out the other side. Her boyfriend from high school, Tom, was on his way to becoming a doctor when his mother was diagnosed with cancer. He had to take time off to care for her, leaving Aimee as the sole breadwinner. As advertised by her pink Polo shirt with the words "Chill Out" embroidered on it, Aimee owns and operates a small frozen yogurt shop nearby. She's in her early thirties and still has the wide-eyed innocence of a child, along with cherubic cheeks that change color like a mood ring. Now that Tom was back and well along in completing his residency, Aimee can relax a little and that respite shows. She's much less fidgety and has stopped crying as much at the least little thing. Like if she accidentally steps on a snail.

"Halsey, say 'hello' to Paula, our newest member. I don't know what we were thinking not inviting her to join from the get-go. Sometimes my brain's as useless as pedals on a wheelchair," said Sally with one of her typical quirky expressions.

"Hi, Paula, so glad you could join us," I said, looking at an earthy momma in her seventies wearing a purple-dyed hemp vest that battled for attention with her rampaging red hair.

Paula gave me a wide grin that turned everything around her from dusky grays to sunflower yellow.

"I am so happy to be included," she said, hoisting a grapevine-made basket onto her lap. "I made some pesto for us from basil I grew at the co-op, and picked a bunch of apricots from my tree."

"Perfect, this will go great with my theme today, which is the start of summer. I've got some grilled pineapple skewers, bruschetta with fresh tomatoes and peach chutney, shrimp satay, and of course, Peggy's crab deviled eggs."

Sally is my best friend here; she is a tall, lean, golden-brown woman in her early sixties, with angular features and elegant long fingers that look like they should be holding a paintbrush in front of an easel overlooking a scenic panorama. Her white hair serves to add a halo around her long neck and jawline. Her lovely oval face and broad smile exude a warm and nurturing aura. Not surprising for a retired nurse, but don't be taken aback at her reaction if someone messes with her. This caregiver has balls.

"Why were you talking about stories when I walked in," I asked, sucking the crab out of an egg white.

My mother taught me better. . . .

"We were talking about the teardown over on the next corner. I spoke to the developer when I was on my walk, and he said that the remodel will have five bedrooms and a basement," Sally explained.

"That's going to be one ugly monster of a house," Aimee said, shaking her head. "It's greed is what it is, that kind of building does not belong here."

"Yes, it worries me that these impersonal behemoth structures are cropping up more and more," said Sally.

"Lots of changes and remodeling going on these days," said Paula, kind of far off. "My new neighbor, a really nice young man, moved in about a month ago. He is doing renovations and also putting in a basement!"

"But I thought that with all the earthquakes we

have, putting in a basement was a dangerous luxury," I questioned.

I'd moved on to the pineapple and forced myself to resist slurping all the juice out first.

"Apparently that is an urban myth. One of Tom's resident friends has one and he says that a basement gives your home the safest level of protection from earthquakes because you have a much stronger foundation for the whole house," Aimee clarified.

"Wow, I want one," said Penelope, thinking.

"Well, here's what I heard," Peggy said with intrigue.

We all leaned in to her.

"You need to have a city-licensed engineer come in first to test and make a soil report before any construction can happen. In the case of the new development we're talking about, I heard from May who lives across the street that they did a pass with their own engineer first, and he suspects that there's oil just about four hundred feet down."

"Just under that one lot?" I asked.

"Don't know, whole thing might be turned into an oil derrick," Peggy answered.

Upon hearing this, I choked on my generous sip of Rosé of Pinot Noir, sending its crisp finish with hints of citrus and sea breeze straight up my nose.

Everyone took a moment to ponder what Peggy had said and to dream about what to do with all the money they would make as oil baronesses.

"You were going to tell us how you hurt your knees, honey," Aimee reminded me.

Like Pavlov's dogs, that was the stimulus the Wine Club girls needed, and they were soon gathered around me. After all there was a dead body involved.

"And Peggy's news is the perfect segue," I said.

"The girls gave me a garden plot up on the hill for my birthday," I explained to Paula.

Her face immediately animated. "I have four plots up there; I grow sweet peas, kale, rhubarb, Brussels sprouts, melons, squash, pineapple, asparagus, and the basil we are enjoying today!"

Okay, right now she looks like she too sprouted from the earth.

"Go on, sugar, tell us your story," Peggy urged.

So I did, leaving out the part about keeping the ring and deed from the detective. Let them think that he has all the evidence. This was a respectable occasion after all, and I'd planned on telling Sally and Peggy later in private.

"Holy dingleberries," Sally said.

So now they've been blessed????

"Does this mean that you could own all the oil under Rose Avenue?" Sally continued.

"I don't know. I have a more pressing issue at the moment, which is convincing the cops that I had nothing to do with the body that Bardot dug up."

"I was thinking you meant ancient bones, are they sure it was a human body?" Peggy asked.

"I saw a hand with bits of flesh still visible." I grimaced.

"Ewwwwww," Aimee said, teary.

"I wonder how long a body can be buried and still not be totally decomposed," Peggy mused.

"Easy enough to find out," Sally said, firing up her smartphone.

"People find bones all the time when working in the gardens," Paula said. "That whole area was farmland, I'm sure cattle and horse carcasses are all over the place."

"But they don't have hands last I checked." Penelope seemed a bit amused by all this.

"Everything hinges on the autopsy results. That'll tell how this person died, and more. Until then my fate is in limbo."

Everyone looked shocked.

"I think that we have the deed to the mineral rights under our house. I'll have to have my husband Max check," said Paula, eying me a little differently now.

"You don't really think that the deed is valid after all those years? I'm sure it has been superseded twenty times over by now," I said.

"I'm real curious about that ring, figuring out the symbols and engravings on that might tell us a whole different story," Penelope mused.

"So what's the plan, Halsey? Tell us what you think we need to do to solve this like you did last time."

"That was way different, Aimee," I said, but my wheels were already spinning.

I glanced over at Peggy and could tell that she was doing the same thing.

"Peggy, you floored me with that story of possible oil under the construction site, do you think that you could follow up on that?"

"Sure, and I'll interrogate, er, quiz May more thoroughly."

"Sally, do you think that you can get more scoop on the developer, if he thinks he's discovered oil, he might be involved somehow, either with the deed or the body. Did you get his name?" I asked.

"Better, I've got his card right here," she said, pulling it out of her back pocket. "Howard T. Platz, it has his cell number too. I'll keep chatting with him."

The rest of the girls were watching me intently.

"Great, Penelope, if I get you photos of the ring, do you think that you could do some research on your museum's database?"

"Good God, of course, and I can access it remotely as well."

I was grateful for her youth and natural born tech savvy.

"Aimee," I said and saw her sit up tall, happy to not be the last team member picked.

"Do you think that during quiet times at your yogurt shop you could do some online research on the history of Rose Avenue and the surrounding area? I'll email you a copy of the deed as well."

"Absolutely, it will be nice to have something to occupy my brain besides sprinkles and freezer levels."

I was mentally trying to come up with something for Paula, but I'd just met her and had no idea what she could do besides grow everything imaginable.

That's when it hit me.

"And Paula, if you would like to help, I wonder if you could get access to records of the last four or five people who have owned my plot? I'll get you the number."

"I know exactly which one is yours, I've had my plots for over thirty years, and I know just who to ask," she said, visibly pleased to be a part of this squad.

"Awesome, meanwhile I'm going to do some checking on the cigar box and see if that turns up any clues. Shall we have a last toast to our plan?"

We all raised our glasses, but before I could say anything else, Paula interrupted me.

"Excuse me, I just thought of something. My husband Max is a member of the local historical society and a few years back he and some others did a whole study on the origins of Rose Avenue."

"I never knew that. I'd love a copy," Sally said still holding her glass in midair.

"I don't know that they kept any. See, they were never able to complete their research. They'd been looking into the story about one of the original landowners being murdered by three 'desperadoes' but they kept coming to dead ends. Either the files were missing or they were under seal," Paula explained.

"Wow, do I smell a connection here?" asked Peggy.

"That's a jump over a very wide creek," said Sally.

"Either way, you should talk to Max. But let me test the waters first. For the longest time he refused to talk about the study."

"Why?" I asked.

"During the time he was working on it a whole string of bad things kept happening to him. First his spare tire was stolen from his truck; next he tripped over an uneven pavement and sprained his ankle. When a dead crow fell from the sky and landed on him in the backyard, he'd had enough and called it quits. All this happened in the same week."

"So does he think he was being haunted by the desperadoes' ghosts?" Peggy asked, skeptical.

"That's exactly what he thinks."

Ay caramba.

Chapter 4

I woke up groggy from a tad too much "Bactine" I'd consumed at Wine Club. I did not want to get out of bed this Saturday morning. The dark and cool cocoon I construct for myself each night was doing its job, and when I tried to sit up, I realized that part of the baggy T-shirt I slept in was weighted down under the body fast asleep next to me.

This is a sign.

I plopped back down, but unfortunately the seal had been broken. I started running through the things I had to do today and knew I'd better get at it.

"Bardot, wake up!"

The lump next to me did not budge. I tried to pull my shirt out from under but got nowhere. The movement caused Bardot to roll further onto it, now on her back with her legs relaxed at her sides. There was no time for this today.

"Bardot! Wake up! I have to get going."

No response. I put my head down next to hers

and staccato-whispered, "Do . . . YOU . . . want . . . your . . . BREAKFAST???"

With that she bolted out of bed, her paws not touching the floor until she was halfway down the hall. I wish that I could be motivated by something so simple.

I had two tasks I needed to accomplish today before I could enjoy a relaxing dinner with Jack. First was to get to the weekly Farmers' Market. Besides securing some of the best produce around, I wanted to talk to a couple of the old timers with a vegetable stand that may know something about the lima bean fields that used to blanket the hill.

I grabbed my market bag, saw that Bardot had scarfed down her food and was stretched out in the morning sun for a postprandial nap, and I headed out. I gasped when I opened the front door and saw Marisol once again perched on my stoop.

"Geez, Marisol, I'm going to have to start charging you rent!"

"Shh, I'm watching that guy."

"Hawaii?"

"No, that one down the street, he's knocking on doors. Sat in his car for the longest time talking on the phone and smoking damn cigarettes."

I looked in that direction and spotted a skinny man wearing a straw derby with a black band walk up to a house. He was carrying a worn leather satchel briefcase. I looked back at Marisol and noticed that she was wearing a baseball cap and sunglasses.

"You're trying to pretend you're me, aren't you?

You want people to think that I'm the neighborhood snoop, not you!"

"I am not," she whispered defiantly. "And keep your voice down, it's Saturday morning, people are trying to sleep."

"You think I don't know what day it is?? I hereby ban you from coming within five feet of my front porch ever again!"

We watched as the man was invited into the house he had approached. I escorted Marisol back to her house leaving no room for argument and told her to do her job and find out who this guy is and what he wants. I saw a glint appear in her eye that told me that she liked this assignment.

The Farmers' Market takes over the land surrounding the community center each Saturday and offers everything from produce to freshly caught fish and seafood, flowers and plants, cheeses, specialty honeys and vinegars and oils, and baked goods. There is always a heightened air of excitement when shoppers discover that the first produce of that season is out. Today, this year's peaches were making their debut.

I was offered a sample as I entered the outdoor row of stalls. It tasted so tangy and sweet and sunny that I had to close my eyes for a second to savor the experience. For some reason that's when I thought about halving them, filling the holes left by the pits with brown sugar and Bourbon, and grilling them.

Do I really need to have alcohol on everything?

The market is truly a family affair and when I

watched one toddler riding in a wagon his dad was pulling, my knees started to sting all over again. To not think about it, I busied myself with picking up the staples for the week: avocados, berries, Santa Barbara mussels, and those yummy peaches. Which is where I ran into Sally.

"I thought about calling you so we could carpool, Halsey, but I've got a tuna boat full of errands to run after this. What's that basket behind you, are those any riper?" Sally asked the merchant.

"No worries. I have a full day too, and in fact this errand has a dual purpose."

I spotted one of the old farmers sitting way in the back of the stall. He was rubbing his hands together to warm them in the morning's cool sea air.

"Excuse me, sir, you look like you could use a cup of coffee," I said to him.

"Boy could I, but I've got to get my old bones working first. I'm getting too old for farmin' and all."

"How about my friend and I treat you and in exchange ask you a few questions about the early days of farming in Mar Vista?"

"Have breakfast with beautiful girls like you two? Heck, I should be the one treating." He grinned.

As Sally went behind the produce table and the farmer pulled up a crate for her to sit on, I headed to the tented food court. I ordered a large coffee for him and two cups of fresh watermelon juice for Sally and myself. It is such a treat; the key is to ask them to use very little ice so you get more juice. I always feign a toothache. . . .

To no surprise, when I returned Sally had the farmer recounting all kinds of tales.

"Curtis was just telling me about how Mar Vista was still very much the Wild West well into the '50s," Sally told me.

We all took a moment to enjoy sips of our drinks.

"My dad grew lima beans and celery up on the hill, people hunted with rifles and bows and arrows, raised poultry, and rode horses up until I was grown and getting ready to ship off to Korea."

"Wow, I can hardly imagine Rose Avenue as rural farmland," I said. "And you took over the business after you returned from the war?" I asked.

"Hah, that's a good one. No way, I'd seen enough of land ownership's bad side as a kid and tried to get as far away from it as I could. Moved to Chicago where we had some relatives."

I looked at Sally who had the same questioning look on her face as I guessed I did.

"Are you referring to crop blights, not enough water, poor soil? That kind of thing?" Sally asked. I suspected that this market was as close as she'd ever been to a farm.

"None of that, the land around here was ideal for growing almost anything. I'm talking about the fighting and backstabbing. Literally. When the Mar Vista pioneers weren't buying land they were selling liquor during Prohibition, running houses of ill repute, and killing each other over the silliest of things."

I let that sink in while he took the final draw

from his coffee cup. I noticed his cracked, stained hands and knew that Curtis hadn't stayed away for long. There was no point in bringing it up, as it would only serve to illuminate his lack of resolve.

"What do you know about Anderson Rose?" I asked, seeing that he was now anxious to get to work selling his harvest.

"Well, now you're talking the big leagues. He was one of the landowners; of course we didn't associate with those highfalutin boys. I remember that he had a dairy; everybody raved about his milk."

"Did he do any drilling or mining, do you know?" Sally had picked up the line of questioning.

"They were all into that, hoping they'd find the Texas tea. That's mostly what they fought over. Funny thing is, if oil had actually been found, there wouldn't be a Mar Vista today. Nobody wants to live around derricks."

He stood up and I knew we were done. We both thanked him and headed to our cars.

"Oh yeah, one more thing," he called out to us. "Rose Avenue was named for Anderson Rose."

Of course it was.

When I got back to the house, I was relieved not to see any sign of Marisol. I wasn't fooled into thinking that she got the message. She was probably just busy wiring some unsuspecting neighbor's house with surveillance cameras.

I joke not.

I noticed a bunch of papers tucked under my doormat. In addition to tree trimmers, upholsterers, and maid service advertisements, there was a group of more official-looking flyers on heavier paper stock.

I grabbed the lot and went inside. I had about an hour before my next errand, so I made myself a cup of tea, and Bardot and I went out back, her to the pool and me to a chaise. I took a lovely sip of my Lady Grey tea with just the right amount of milk and sugar. The marine layer was burning off and the sun was spotlighting everything in Technicolor. All was right with the world.

I opened one of the fancy flyers.

> **Mr. Bobby Snyder, Esq., Mineral Rights Agent**
> *Do you know if you own the rights to the precious five hundred feet under your home?*
> *"Mineral rights" refers to subsurface rights to any mineral, such as natural gas and oil. However, it also includes all minerals found beneath the land's surface, such as gold, diamonds, quartz, and copper.*
> **Oil and minerals have been found in your area!**
> *Call today for a consultation, and let your house pay for itself.*

Seriously? I made a mental note to follow up with Aimee and her research on the deed.

Bardot, Penelope, and I walked down the hill of the Santa Monica airport complex to the area dedicated for the afternoon's Flea Market. Since she was relatively new to the neighborhood, I'd suspected that she hadn't yet been to one and being an art lover, she'd appreciate it. Not that this market held a trove of objets d'art. It was a bit of everything; Indian fabric pants, shawls and dresses, pet hair pick up devices, frogs carved in marble, copper, wood, etc., advertising and brand name memorabilia, even a place that sold steamed corn on a stick.

But I was there to find old cigar tins.

"This is so much fun, Halsey, thank you for inviting me. I'm used to the British ones, but it is exciting to see all this Americana." Penelope beamed. "Ooh look, are those things all salt and pepper shakers?" she asked, pointing to a table of Bob's Big Boy Burger figurines.

"I'm afraid so," I said, eyeing another table of taxidermy freaks of the animal kingdom. When Bardot started to pull me toward the two-headed rabbit, I suggested that we turn down another path.

We walked past a stand selling '70s' Polaroid cameras, tape decks, and projectors. "Good God you Americans save everything, don't you?"

"An overstuffed garage or attic, it's our 'get rich quick' scheme. Speaking of, did you get a flyer today from a mineral rights lawyer or agent?"

"You must mean Bobby Snyder, yes? He actually paid me a visit this morning. He's a funny chap, wears a straw bowler."

"Ha-ha funny or peculiar?" I asked.

"The latter, and he believes that we're all going to be massively rich."

The vendors were organized by theme, and we

had come into the general area where I'd hoped to find cigar items. Here, they were selling pricey vintage items: old Coca-Cola wooden crates and boxes, porcelain advertising signs, and luggage from the 1900s.

"So strange, I've never heard anyone talk about oil or mineral rights since I moved here, and now it seems to be cropping up all over the place. I think I'll call Mr. Snyder tomorrow and find out just what sort of consulting he does," I said.

All of a sudden Bardot jumped four feet in the air and tried to cling to me. Instead, she knocked both of us down to the ground. I looked over to an array of very old toys and spied the culprit. Bardot had stuck her nose where it didn't belong and had accidentally freed one of the creepiest jack-in-the-box clowns I'd ever seen. Its eyes were meant to look like daisies or some other flower with blue petals all around them. But it came off as some kind of mutant Smurf with vitiligo.

Why did it have to be clowns?

From the ground, I saw that a few yards ahead was indeed a blanket upon which sat a display of cigar tins and boxes. Penelope helped me to my feet and we headed over to it. I located the photo on my phone of the old "La Union" tin that I'd dug up and approached the vendor.

Boy, I can't wait to sit down to a nice dinner.

The "provenance" of my cigar tin I learned, dated back to the late 1800s or early 1900s. Despite the Spanish name for the cigars, our expert suspected that this item's country of origin was most likely England where he knew that tobacconists of the time sold such cigars.

"Every answer seems to prompt a whole new set of questions," I said to Penelope after we'd thanked the tin seller and were heading back home.

"That's the nature of the beast when it comes to antiques, luv. Which reminds me, I have an associate at the museum who specializes in rare and historical jewelry. I'd be happy to have him take a look at the ring you found."

"That would be awesome. Didn't you get the photos of the ring I sent you?"

"Yes, I did. But he'll want to see the real thing, test the metal, really examine the engravings."

How does she know I've still got the ring? I told them I turned everything over. "I'll get it to you. Okay?"

"Lovely."

It really wasn't "okay" or "lovely." I hated to let it out of my sight, but I really didn't have a good enough reason to say no.

Chapter 5

"What do you mean, 'we have to run an errand first,' and why are there still dogs in your truck?" I asked in a little more of a whine than I would have liked.

"Relax, honey, we will be sitting at a romantic candlelit table for two in no time. Besides, I'm delivering the dogs for a CARA rescue, so it's for a good cause," Jack calmly explained.

I'd best explain. Jack is a certified dog search and rescue instructor with CARA, the Canine Rescue Association. He runs field trials in the Santa Monica Mountains with handler and dog teams, preparing them for the real thing. Like when a hiker has fallen into a rock crevice or a small plane has gone down. He has worked with Bardot and claims that she's a natural, something that I was skeptical of until she actually saved my life. I'll tell you about it sometime.

Technically he's on call 24/7, and since I've known Jack, he has assisted in ten successful rescues, people in all kinds of bad situations. So, yes, this is a good thing.

I calmed myself, a little. I was still disappointed. After a tough day, I'd decided to do it up for tonight; I thought that I might start with a martini, just to get my groove back. Heck, I'd even put on a dress. But before you think that I looked like Cinderella going to the ball, I'll set you straight. I chose a blue and white sleeveless floral number along with a denim fitted jacket. Gladiator sandals completed the ensemble. To his credit, Jack had changed into a green and white striped button-down and crisp beige linen pants, so the evening did show *some* promise.

"I still don't like showing up to a nice restaurant in this huge truck," I said, my temper softening.

"Don't worry, Halsey, we won't be."

"What do you mean, and why are we turning into the Santa Monica airport?"

"The errand, remember?"

"You didn't tell me that the errand involved air travel!"

"Well, now you know," he said, laughing.

We pulled up to an electric gate on the south side of the runway and Jack reached out and punched in a key code. A moment later, the gate swung open and we proceeded onto the runway area. The sun was waning and casting a striation of vermillion and orange colors across the horizon.

This is actually the perfect time for a plane ride.

Midway down the runway toward the western end of the airport a small prop plane was starting up. We parked just behind it in front of a hangar.

"Come on, we've got no time to waste if we want to enjoy the full beauty of this sunset," Jack said, coaxing the dogs out of their crates in the back of his truck. "You remember Neil, Halsey? He took you on your first CARA training drop."

"How could I forget?" I said, waving to Neil who had started up the plane for us.

After Jack had loaded the dogs onto the plane, he and Neil went through a preflight check. Which gave me time to reminisce about the first time I'd flown with Jack. It was our makeup date after a rocky start, and he definitely wanted to make an impression. He told me a little about what to expect, but left out some key parts, like we were both going to be lowered from a helicopter into the forest and create confusing scents for dog and handler teams that were on a tracking mission. It's not so much that I'm afraid of heights, I'm more afraid of surprises. He hadn't told me what we were doing until I was strapped to him and we jumped out the door. He did atone with a beautiful picnic lunch of bread, cheeses, and a lovely Pinot Gris from Alsace. But it would have been nice to know in advance.

Just like today.

I took the copilot seat, strapped in, and put on my headset. Jack communicated with the tower and we taxied to our takeoff position, which was facing the western sunset.

"Okay, Halsey, time to go house hunting," Jack said as we leveled off and headed up the coast. It was a clear evening and we were flying low enough to get a really good look at the privileged Malibu proprietors and their manses.

There are no tall buildings in the 'Bu as they call it. So the view was of white sandy beaches that were pretty much empty at this hour. As we flew over the Santa Monica pier and its giant Ferris wheel, we headed north parallel to Pacific Coast Highway. After we passed the sign declaring MALIBU, 27 MILES OF SCENIC BEAUTY, the homes below got impressively more majestic.

"Which one is Sting's again?" I asked, surveying the multi-leveled, multi-styled ocean front homes. Cape Cod this was not but I was enjoying myself imagining the possibilities all the same. The next extra eight million dollars I have is going to one of these. Better make it ten million, I know I'll have to remodel.

"Would you look at that sky? This just never gets old," Jack said, taking in a breath. Jack has a lot of Zen-like qualities and he really does appreciate nature in all its forms. He also has an amazing ability to fall asleep, even if just for five minutes anywhere. This is SO annoying and I'm SO jealous.

When we landed in Santa Barbara, my mind started running through all the wonderful restaurants that I'd read about. Were we going to The Lark, trendy but also serving delicious farm and ocean specialties? Or maybe he'd opted for artisanal Italian at Olio e Limone. He could also be kicking it old school with the 1920s hillside El Encanto for a romantic dinner on the terrace.

Or not.

The person who met us to claim the dogs had us follow him to the parking lot. There, in addition to his truck was parked an old Harley-Davidson motorcycle. He put his dogs in the truck and handed Jack the keys and two helmets.

"Just leave the bike back here and take the keys and helmets into the office. They'll hold them for me."

Jack thanked the man and turned to me grinning from ear to ear.

"Oh no, Mr. Jack Thorton, I am not getting on that thing. Because number one, I am wearing a dress in case you hadn't noticed."

"I'd noticed."

"And two, I am not pulling up to a nice restaurant on a beat-up old bike, it's worse than the truck."

It didn't take us long to get to the center of town, and from the little I could see behind Jack's massive back, we were not heading toward the coast. I held onto him with one arm while I used the other in a futile effort to keep my dress from blowing up. From the honks we kept hearing, I intuited that I had not been successful.

I was still so mad at him that I pretty much buried my face into his back and gave him nips now and then to remind him that Halsey was not amused. When we finally stopped, I looked down to the ground and saw that we were sitting atop a weedy, cracked pavement. The bike suddenly tilted drastically to port side and I would have fallen to the ground if Jack hadn't caught me. I guess this was where we were dining tonight.

As we walked up to the turquoise blue and white shack Jack tried to explain.

"This may look like a roadside taco stand but I can assure you it's not. And if you don't believe me, you can ask Julia Child, she discovered this hole-in-the-wall and was their biggest fan."

"Um, pretty sure I won't be able to ask her. . . ."

We walked in past the griddle, grill, and menu boards to where a woman was pounding masa into balls and then flattening it in a tortilla press. Jack explained to the grumbling crowd that we were meeting friends. We passed through the other end and into the "dining room." (Picture plastic chairs and simple tables under the same turquoise trim and white tent-like room.)

"There he is," Jack said, pointing to a table in the back corner.

There sat quite a peculiar man waving to us and gesturing to what seemed to be an array of everything that was on the menu. The man was wearing a suit, white shirt, and bow tie and looked like he belonged here about as much an astronaut would. He was short and round and wore his meager hair in an Albert Einstein firework.

Maybe he rode in on a motorcycle too. . . .

Jack steered me to the table and whispered, "You're going to love him." Then he turned back to the man.

"Halsey, let me introduce you to Mr. Frederick Ott, friend, genius, and early California historian."

"Mr. Jack tends to err on the side of hyperbole, I

am certainly no genius. But I am charmed to be dining with such a lovely lady, do sit down," he said in an accent that wasn't quite German.

"Very nice to meet you, Mr. Ott; do you share Jack's interesting taste in restaurants?"

"Please call me Frederick, and don't judge a book by its cover. My wife and I have been making a pilgrimage up here for almost twenty years, kind of ironic for an old Swiss, no? I am lucky today as I just happen to be in Santa Barbara for an estate appraisal."

"Thank you for ordering for us, everything looks divine. And I brought a little something to accompany the meal," Jack said, producing a bottle of Bistro Classic Paso Robles Zinfandel.

Surprise number four, but this one I like.

"I won't be drinking, since I'm driving and flying, but you two please enjoy."

Next out of Jack's pocket came a votive candle that he lit while giving me a wink.

"Lovely, let's eat first before the food gets cold and then we can discuss this fascinating piece of parchment that Jack tells me you plucked from the ground."

We spent the next thirty minutes feasting on dishes I couldn't pronounce and certainly had never tasted before. I think my favorite was something called Lomita Suizo, grilled marinated pork with melted cheese between two corn tortillas and topped with the freshest pico de gallo I'd ever had. The tortillas melted in your mouth.

I quit after that and before the men did, so Frederick thought it was time that I showed him the deed while he ate. I had loaded all the photos I'd taken on my iPhone and took him through a slide show of the front, back, and close-ups of the document.

He didn't say a thing for the longest time. When he had taken his last bite, he thoroughly wiped his mouth and hands with a wad of napkins from the dispenser on the table.

"And Jack tells me you also found a ring," he finally said. "May I possibly see some photos?"

I complied, and once again he carefully studied them. "This ring, is it very heavy?"

"I would say that it feels like the weight of about half a roll of quarters, if that makes sense."

"Perfectly."

"Do you have any ideas, Frederick?" Jack asked.

"Hmmm," he said, closing his eyes to think. "First off I'd say it's a safe bet the two items will either validate each other or prove them to be imposters. The provenance will be critical."

"This is a signet ring, correct?" I asked.

"Undoubtedly. It was historically used as a seal and featured a unique family crest, emblem, or monogram. Often passed from father to son and so on, the ring was used to sign legal or important documents. By dipping the ring into melted wax, it left a distinct seal that was considered to be more official than a signature. The ring was designed in mirrored image to ensure it came out properly when leaving its mark."

"So this ring is clearly an antique?" I asked.

"Nothing is clear in the world of antiquity, dear Halsey, until it is proven."

Okay, that's the second time today that I've been told this. How does the saying go? *Those who cannot remember the past are condemned to repeat it.*

"I understand. If, hypothetically, the ring was authenticated, what would you guess is the age of it?"

"Victorian, I'd say late 1800s. Were there any other interesting aspects to the ring that you noted when you examined it, Halsey?"

"There was an inscription on the inner side of the band, it read 'Memento Mori.' "

I studied his face for a change of expression. After a few moments he nodded slowly.

"Anything else?"

"Not that I saw, but I really haven't had the time to give it a full inspection. I'd planned to do so this weekend."

"It is my strongest recommendation that you don't touch the item again until you find a jewelry expert who can handle it correctly."

"Okay, you're scaring me now. It has a curse, doesn't it?"

Even Jack looked a little concerned and moved in closer.

"I have no idea, but I strongly suspect that this is indeed a poison locket signet ring."

Why couldn't I have found a Buffalo head nickel like everyone else does?

It was close to midnight when Jack and I arrived back at the homestead. The plan was formed that we would take Bardot for a quick constitutional around the block, then crash, sleep in, and enjoy a lazy Sunday morning. This date was getting better for me.

Unfortunately, in the darkness we hadn't noticed the black and white parked across the street until we heard two car doors open. I looked in that direction and saw Augie and a uniformed officer approaching.

Am I ever going to get a break? And I don't mean a Kit Kat bar.

"Did I not tell you to stay close to home, Halsey?" Augie looked at his watch with a sour face.

"I have. What are you now, the curfew enforcement police? I know I don't look it, but I'm pretty sure that I'm over twenty-one."

I was going for "pleasantly haughty."

We'd stopped at a bar on the way back to the airport in Santa Barbara and Frederick had talked me into doing tequila shots with him. That old Swiss can hold his liquor, he must have learned to drink as a boy from a rescue Saint Bernard with a mini keg tied around his neck in the Alps. In either case, I was a tad "in my cups."

"Officer Cruz and I are here to escort you to the station," Augie replied with cold eyes.

"Hey, hey, that's not necessary," Jack intervened. "I'm the one responsible for keeping her out so late, take me to the station."

Just when I thought that the situation couldn't get any more ridiculous, guess who joined the party?

"If you guys gonna talk outside all night and wake up the street, then I'd better put on coffee," Marisol said from her doorstep waving us in.

"Sorry, Auntie," Augie said when we were all situated in Marisol's living room.

I'd been in her inner sanctum sanctorum once or twice before, but at this time of night it all looked like Grandma's cozy sitting room.

You don't fool me, Marisol.

Over a worn in but comfortable-looking sofa sat an afghan blanket that appeared to have been crocheted by loving hands. Photos of happy family events over the years lined the wall and souvenirs from trips to Disneyland took the top shelf of a wooden cabinet.

The room's illumination came primarily from her large, newest model TV that looked impressive but would certainly draw no red flags to the uninitiated. I on the other hand, knew that this was the headquarters for "spy central." In an emergency, she used that screen to access spy cameras her godson had installed for her around her house and who knows whom else's. I watched as Office Cruz took in the room and saw evidence pointing to what Augie had certainly told him, "I have a dear, old Auntie Marisol."

Augie assumed position on the master club chair.

"We now have an ID on the body from the gardens," he began.

Marisol didn't even feign an effort to go make coffee when she heard this. She pulled the ottoman away from Augie's chair and plunked herself down for story time.

"Her name is Abigail Rose," he continued. "She went missing about a year ago, at the time she was ninety and suffering from dementia. We did a thorough search and when nothing turned up, we concluded that she'd probably wandered off and soon after died."

"I remember her," Marisol said, "crusty old thing, always getting into everybody's business."

All four of us looked at her and stared with disbelief.

"A fox always smells her own hole." I thought I'd said only in my head. From the looks I now got, apparently not.

"How tragic," Jack said. "I hope that she didn't die alone."

"There was at least one other person with her at the time around her death," Officer Cruz said and then paused to let the suspense build, "the one who buried her up on the hill."

"Halsey, I looked through our records; you must recall that Mrs. Rose disappeared shortly after you moved into your house."

"I remember people talking about it, but I'd never even seen her. That was her house on the other side of Paula's, right? That's almost a block away from me."

"You and your dog seem to get around fine all over the neighborhood," he said.

"Please, Augie, you're being ridiculous. If you recall at the time, you all were busy falsely accusing me of killing someone else. I'm really a great multi-tasker but double murders in the same week is way above my pay grade."

In situations of fear, anger, or just plain rudeness, I tend to err on the sarcastic side.

"Maybe so, but you should know from experience that this puts you right back on the squad's radar," Augie informed me. "Again, stay close to home while we work the evidence and until we get the autopsy report."

"I guess eloping to Cuba will have to wait," I said to Jack. He looked at me with wide, hopeful eyes, and I realized that from now on I should carry a sign that says "sarcasm" to flash at moments like this.

Chapter 6

Wine Club was held at Paula's this time around. And as she boasted, it was going to feature guest speakers.

We met in the backyard of her house, where there was ample comfortable seating and tables under a light canopy to diffuse the sun. Beyond the patio and grill area, an extraordinary panoply of nature's bounty waited to be enjoyed.

I must have counted five fruit trees, all in full blossom or ready for picking. I noticed a banana tree in the back corner, weighted down with bunches of ripening green fruit, naturally prepackaged for portability. And in the other back corner, I think I'll dub it "the back 40," were rows of fruits and vegetables growing on vines.

"Did you say that you have several plots up on the hill as well?" I asked Paula while surveying her own yard.

"Yes," she said, giggling as we all settled in comfortably around the table.

"Paula's one of those plant freaks," said Peggy, teasing her. "All this fresh healthy food, what's a girl got to do to get a Twinkie around here?"

"Well, for one thing, I don't think that it would pair well with this Sea Smoke 'Botella' Pinot Noir I'm pouring," said Paula.

"Yum, I taste fresh earth, blueberries, and licorice," Sally said, not prepared to wait for everyone to toast.

"Sounds delish," said Penelope. "How do you lot know so much about wines? In the pubs back home, it's pretty much down to three choices, red, white, or a pint."

"We go through a lot of hit or miss; if it's good we take our time and savor the taste, if it's just so-so, we tend to drink it more quickly. And it has nothing to do with price," I explained.

"Over time our palates seem to have gotten in sync," Sally added.

"So have our periods," Aimee said, arriving a tad late.

We all laughed and then those her statement still applied to started doing the math.

"Here's a glass for you, Aimee. Peggy, please take an endive leaf filled with salmon mousse and pass the tray," Paula directed.

"I like this wine, I'm getting currants, cherry, and smoke," Aimee concluded.

I thought it tasted like the soothing of a warm bath after a long day of skiing, but what do I know?

"Halsey, before I bring out our guest speakers, do you have any news for us on your garden findings?" Paula was in charge today it seemed.

"Wait," interrupted Aimee. "I actually have an announcement to make."

"How dramatic," Sally said. "Does it concern the regularity of our bowel movements? Because it is widely known in the medical journals that women who—"

"Stop!" Peggy shouted. "We can do without the scatological theories."

Okay, I'm going to have to look that up.

"No, it has nothing to do with any of, um, those things. You guys know that since Halsey helped us build a website and do promotions for Chill Out that business has really picked up. So much so that I've been able to hire two more people."

We all stood up and applauded as Aimee did her customary crying. It was a happy cry.

"Soooo," she continued, "this gives me a chance to get more experience in the food industry. To-morrow I start a six-week baking and pastry class. I really want to be able to add healthy but also deli-cious items to our shop's menu."

Once again we stood up and applauded.

"You are going to be famous." I beamed at her.

"Thank you, Halsey. This means that after today I won't be able to attend many Wine Club meet-ings, but I did get some research done on the his-tory of Rose Avenue, and with Paula we organized today's presenters."

I started to look for the curtain from which the Wizard would appear.

"I do have some things to update you on," Aimee continued, "but maybe we should do that at the end."

"Agreed," sanctioned Peggy. "And I too have news about the rumors of underground oil being found at that massive new construction site."

Paula dipped her head into her house and said in an audible whisper, "We're ready for you. What? Well, just set it to record and come on out!"

It was clear that Paula was counting on this to be her first big moment with the Wine Club.

"Allow me to present two esteemed members of the Rose Avenue & Environs Historical Society, my husband Max Adler and his new associate Malcolm Abernathy."

Once again we stood and applauded, and I mentally checked my cardio for today off my list.

Max looked like a diehard beatnik. He sported a pork pie hat, walked barefoot, and was clearly relaxed in his tall, lanky frame. He had warm eyes and a big smile that was in full bloom as he took center stage on the patio.

"Well, hello," he said in a melodic voice that sounded like a cross between Burl Ives and Seal. "My wife tells me that you are interested in the history of Rose Avenue."

"The area in general," Paula said, nodding to us and hoping we would follow suit.

"Okay then, let's start with the provenance of the area. The land was originally occupied by what we call 'California Rancheros,' men of Spanish and Mexican descent who mostly raised cattle. About the time that the Mexican War was ending, Yankee immigrants were making their way across the country attracted by the discovery of gold here."

His easy, professorial approach was certainly drawing me in, but I needed to focus him to give us facts more germane to my mysterious cigar box and its contents.

"Excuse me, Max, my name is Halsey. This is so fascinating, don't you all agree? I wonder if you could tell us a bit about Anderson Rose. Did he own all the land around us? And was he also mining for gold?"

"Perfect segue, Halsey. He was one of said Yankee pioneers. Shortly after he arrived, he began acquiring land. Some say over the years thousands of acres. He did initially mine, but with poor results, so he stuck to ranching."

"What about oil, Max? Was he doing any drilling?" Peggy asked and we all snapped to attention.

"Best to let young Malcolm answer that, he is indeed the expert on this subject."

I hadn't really noticed much about him up to now, but when he traded places with Max, I did my customary once over. He kind of looked like a cross between Harry Potter and the kid Sherman in the *Mr. Peabody* cartoons. Only grown up, mostly. He was a redhead with rampaging hair that took off in all directions.

"Good afternoon, ladies," he said, soft-spoken.

I looked over at Sally and Peggy, who both looked like they wanted to adopt him. I then noticed that they would have to fight off Paula first.

"The discovery of oil in Los Angeles at the turn of the century and the fight for ownership is the stuff of legends," he said, sounding like he'd practiced this.

He gave a light cough that made his milk and honey complexion go crimson. I doubted that he'd ever seen so many women at one time, let alone talked to all of them. The only one who wasn't enraptured by this boy was Penelope, who seemed to be preoccupied with checking her emails.

"Go on, honey," Aimee encouraged.

"You may recall the film, *There Will Be Blood* with Daniel Day-Lewis? Adapted from the book, *Oil*, by Upton Sinclair?"

Crickets. This was more of a *Magic Mike* crowd.

"I've seen it," said Paula enthusiastically.

Nobody likes a suck-up. . . .

"Any-hoo," said Penelope, looking bored and now inspecting her manicure for chips.

"Well, it's a story that played out over and over back then and it shows how the competitive lust for finding and claiming the most oil drives people into moral bankruptcy."

"So is there oil underground here or not?" Peggy asked. She was getting impatient and Paula had stopped pouring.

"We may never know," Malcolm hesitantly responded, fearing Peggy's wrath.

"Sweet Jesus on a moped, why can't we find out?" Sally was also losing patience.

"The reason we can't be certain one way or the other," Malcolm said, his cheeks now the color and vibrancy of cherry lights on a cop car, "is because they weren't able to drill deep enough. By mandate they could only drill to a certain depth, and when that yielded no results, they moved on to other money-making endeavors."

"Oh, there's oil down there," Max said.

"How can you be so sure?" I asked.

"Because I've seen it with my own eyes," he replied and disappeared into the house. When we heard the TV go on it was clear that class had been dismissed.

"And the other wonderful news," Paula said, trying to recapture her audience, "is that Malcolm is now our next-door neighbor!"

Applause erupted all around, mostly.

Paula was squeezing and hugging him so tightly that I fully expected his eyes to pop out like a Panic Pete squeeze toy.

It was odd, I thought, that someone so young, working as an historian for a small community group, could afford a house so close to the beach. And didn't Paula say that he was also putting in a basement?

There's more to this story.

Malcolm finally wriggled free and Wine Club was adjourned.

The next morning greeted me with beautiful sunshine and temperatures in the low 70s. Bardot and I decided that the conditions were perfect for a brisk walk around the 'hood. I grabbed a fresh peach from my farmers' market trove and slowly opened the door. I was expecting to find Marisol outside and was going to unload on her. But all was quiet on my porch, so we headed down the block.

For a brief moment, I felt some concern for her; after all, I was the one who sent her on a mission to find out what Mr. Bobby Snyder, Esq. was up to. As I passed her big front window, I saw a shutter slat lift letting in sunlight that reflected off her gold tooth.

Silly me, she was up to her old tricks.

I spotted Peggy talking to Sally in front of her house, and we crossed over.

"There's my favorite pooch," cooed Peggy as she plopped to the ground to snuggle with Bardot. My dog's response was to roll on her back and do serpentine moves with her hips while airing out her hoohaw.

Bardot is what you might call a free spirit.

"We were just about to visit the construction site of that house they're working on. The one where they claim they hit oil while digging. Want to tag along?" Sally asked.

"Heck yeah," I said. Peggy donned her pith helmet (there's a story there but none of us have been brave enough to ask) and led the way.

A stroll along Rose Avenue is always like a tonic to me. Every house tells a story, both by its appearance and by signs of human presence all around it. A small soccer goal net and an array of different sized balls on one lawn indicate that this sport is a family affair. At another, the sight of both the United States and Marine Corps flags flying tells of their patriotism. Collectively the homes on Rose

Avenue speak of lives well lived, of fun had, and of growing families.

We rounded the corner and walked over to the next street that was parallel to Rose. The corner lot was blocked from sight with covered wire fencing. From above it, we could see the beginnings of the framing but little else. The requisite port-o-potty sat at one end of the lot. You would think that that alone would provide enough incentive to try and finish if not early, then at least on time. We could hear raised voices coming from the other side of the fence. So needless to say we got closer and quiet so that we could eavesdrop.

"I can't accept that as collateral. You can't prove that you own the rights to whatever's under here, which is probably nothing. Besides, I heard that everything belongs to Rose, so you need to pay me what you owe me!"

We looked at each other. This was more than we'd bargained for.

"Helloooo," Sally bravely cooed. Being the tallest among us, she could just barely see over the top of the fence.

The shouting stopped and moments later we watched a laborer exit through the gate in the fence. He quickly got into his truck and sped away.

"Do I have visitors?" we heard a different voice ask.

"Hi, Howard," Sally said. "Remember me?"

"Of course," he said, joining us on the sidewalk while quickly closing the gate. "And you've brought friends, welcome."

Bardot emitted a low guttural noise, a sign that

she wasn't all too agreeable with our selection of this guy as a friend.

We introduced ourselves. Howard was a jolly-looking guy, the corners of his mouth naturally turned up and his eyebrows arched when he talked. I guessed that he was somewhere in his middle to late sixties. He wore a button-down shirt and khakis, and though his sleeves were rolled up, his manicured hands betrayed any idea that he participated in manual labor.

"I'm afraid that the site is too dangerous right now, otherwise I'd invite you in. Give me a few weeks and I should be able to give you the grand tour," he explained.

"We're all intrigued by the idea of adding a basement, this is the second one we've heard of," I said.

"Yes, I don't know why people see this as such a novel idea. A finished basement adds so much space for, say, a kid's playroom, a screening room, or the traditional bar and games area."

"Rumor has it that you've found oil not too far down," Peggy said, getting down to business.

Howard studied her for a moment and then laughed.

"Rumor is the correct word for it, we really have very little to substantiate that claim at the moment. This is more of an off-handed comment getting blown out of proportion. Don't get me wrong, striking oil would be a blessing from the heavens, but I'm not counting on it. I'm just happy that I thought to secure the mineral rights when I bought the property to develop."

I need to look at that deed again and see how wide an area it covers.

One look at Peggy and I could see that she wasn't buying his vague response.

"So in digging the basement, you haven't found any sign of oil?" Peggy asked.

"Just dirt and old roots. Say you look familiar. Have I ever done any work for you?" Howard asked.

"No."

"You sure? I know, I'll bet it was when I was a teenager. I used to apprentice for a contractor named Sam during the summers."

"Sure, I know Sam. He built our extra bedroom and addition when the kids kept coming."

Peggy was softening.

"I remember that your house was always neat as a pin, which was mind-boggling. It seemed that all the neighborhood kids came to your house to play. Or, it might have been because of those home-made cookies that appeared out of the oven every afternoon," Howard said, his face all lit up.

"Sam called them little discs of delight," Peggy cooed.

Shoot, was Howard playing her?

I glanced over at Sally, but she seemed enchanted with Howard as well. Perhaps I'd just eaten an extra bowl of cynicism that morning.

Chapter 7

When Bardot and I returned home, Marisol, who was sitting on my front steps, greeted us.

"I have a restraining order, I swear," I said as I sat down next to her.

"Who's going to execute it, Augie?" She laughed.

The self-appointed "Mayor of Rose Avenue" loved to flaunt that she had the cops in her back pocket.

"You been over to that damn construction site?"

I felt around my clothes and hair, trying to find the bug she must have planted on me. When I came up empty, I started frisking Bardot.

"We talked to the developer, yes. But he wouldn't let us see anything."

"You got to go at night, when nobody's around."

"Have you done that?"

She shook her head, but I wasn't convinced.

"So what have you found out about Mr. Bobby Snyder? And don't tell me about what he says he's doing, I've read the flyer."

She looked to both sides to check if anyone else was listening.

Really?

"I told you he smokes, right?"

"So?"

"So he drops his goddamn butts out his car window onto the street."

"He's a pig, that's all you've got?" This was going nowhere.

"For now," she said, but she was grinning.

"Come on, Bardot. I actually have a job, and must get to work," I said mostly to Marisol.

"I'll know a lot more in a couple of days," she added as I unlocked my front door.

"Spill," I said, rejoining her on the stoop.

"I put one of those butts in a baggie and gave it to Augie. He's running DNA on it."

"How did you convince Augie to do it? You had better not have brought up my name in connection with this, I'm already in enough hot water as you saw last night."

"You're right, you're in deep doo-doo."

"I can't image that he can have the lab run random tests for no reason."

"I gotta go," she said and disappeared.

I gotta lie down. . . .

It was time for me to start doing some research on the deed, Abigail Rose, and anything else I could think of to get me off the suspect list. I did a quick run through of my emails, returned a call from my Coast Guard client, who wants to add to their website (billable hours, yay!), and pulled out the cigar box. With what I had learned from Frederick about the deed and ring's possible value, I was now hiding the tin in a moderately secret place. *I need to find a safer alternative*, I thought.

I delicately took out the yellowed document and laid it on my desk. It appeared to be on legal-sized paper and was being employed horizontally. There was printing and writing on both sides and it was scored accordion-style in four places. I didn't attempt to fold it but imagined that when it was it would have fit nicely into a man's inside jacket breast pocket.

The deed was issued by the West Republic Land & Title Company, which seemed like as good a place as any to start. The business is now defunct, but my search led me to the USC archives, where I was at least able to view similar documents from that company. This one was pretty much a match. But when I drilled down and added the name "Anderson Rose" to my search, I came up empty. It was time to set up a query script and let it do the work. While I was at it, I created one for Abigail Rose as well.

Just as I launched it, there was a knock on my office side door. I was going to ignore it and pack away my artifacts, but Bardot stood on her back legs at the window to the street and wagged her tail intensely. I peeked out behind her and saw Malcolm waiting by the door.

He seems harmless enough.

I tossed the jacket from the back of my chair over everything on my desk.

"Hello, I do hope that I'm not interrupting your work. I was heading to the gardens and remembered you telling me that this was your office," he explained at the threshold.

"Not at all, come in."

I saw him take a quick look over my shoulder to my computer screen.

"Would you like some water?" I asked, quickly ushering him toward the small kitchen at the opposite end of the room. When I looked back, the screen had thankfully gone into sleep mode.

He chose coconut water and then we sat at the conference table in the middle of the room. I made sure that his back was to my desk.

"I was fascinated by your talk the other day, but I wondered what got you started on the history of our little community? You're so young; wouldn't you rather be exploring the world?"

His cheeks went as orange as tungsten lightbulbs. "My family was among the first settlers in America and they go back all the way to the *Mayflower*. Eventually a few headed west, not so much for gold, but for land. My parents both died when I was young, drunk driver."

"Oh God, I'm so sorry."

He gave me a slight smile. "I was raised in a series of foster homes here in California, and it was only natural that I wanted to trace back my heritage. I started in the Bay Area, which is where I was born, and a series of discoveries has led me down to Southern California."

"So you have no relatives nearby? What about on the East Coast?"

"None that are living, I'm afraid. So here I am, I get a stipend from the historical society, and I work as an archivist at UCLA."

Still doesn't explain the house. . . .

I started to wonder why he was telling me all this and hoped he wasn't getting the wrong idea. I had absolutely no interest in him personally. But Bardot seemed to like him and was sitting calmly, watching him. It may have been because she'd never seen a ginger before. . . .

He checked himself as he started to turn around and look at my desk. I wasn't ready to reveal my find to him just yet, even if Paula and Max endorsed him. After all, I'd just met *them*.

"You said that you are on your way to the gardens, do you have a plot up there?" I asked.

"Me? No, I would love to have one, I hope someday, but you must know how coveted they are. And you?"

"Funnily enough the Wine Club ladies procured one for my birthday. Someone knew someone who dated someone who heard about a lone patch that had been left unclaimed and unattended." With those last words, I noticed his expression change ever so slightly.

"Look at the time," he said suddenly. "It was lovely to visit with you and your dog, but I must be off. Thanks ever so for the water."

With that he disappeared. Not quite as magical as Marisol but he was gone all the same. Bardot sniffed the chair he had been in and gave me a questioning look.

Just then my computer monitor came back to life meaning that one of my queries had come back with some information. I went back to my desk to take a look. Bardot went outside to nap in the lounge chair.

When I sat down, I saw that the return was for the Abigail Rose search. I'd set up some pretty strict parameters for this. Mostly I was interested in Abigail's relatives, last known addresses, that sort of thing. I clicked on the link to Intelius, a good website resource for people searches, background checks, and such. The page that loaded offered three matches:

Christopher B. Rose, Bronxville, NY
Burton E. Macgregor, Palm Coast, FL
Michael P. Abernathy, San Francisco, CA

Could it be? I followed the links for the Abernathy listing. The site teases you just enough to tell you it has what you are looking for, but stops short of turning over that info until you choose one of their plans and request a report. For about three dollars I'd hoped I would find something I could use.

Boy, did I.

About two minutes later I received the report via email. I opened it and scrolled down through a litany of caveats, source references, and birth records. It seems that Michael, now deceased, was the grandson of one Abigail Rose of Mar Vista, CA. He never married and had one sibling, Charles, who had died in his late twenties.

Charles had to have been Malcolm's father. Making Abigail his great-grandmother!

Chapter 8

Wow.

Suddenly I didn't want to be in my office anymore, especially since Malcolm knew that I was here alone. Why was he hiding his identity?

I needed to clear my mind and not jump to conclusions. I decided that Bardot and I would take a late afternoon stroll.

To try and stay out of Marisol's line of sight, we avoided going past her house and went the other way around the block. We watched kids in uniforms arrive home from school. There were housekeepers and day nurses hiking a path up the hill to catch the bus. And the gardeners were on their last lawn for the day. Since this was a less common path for us, Bardot was taking extra time with the smells and messages left by other dogs. This was like coming upon a Facebook page for a name from the past and wanting to see every picture, read every post, and analyze all their friends. Only in dog language.

The walk was definitely helping. If I could tie Abigail to Malcolm that quickly, surely the cops had as well. And they could access real estate records instantly, so I was sure that they knew about Malcolm inheriting her estate. Something obvious must have ruled him out as a suspect or Augie would have told me. Still, it wouldn't explain why he was lying to all of us.

Wait! What about all the obvious things that rule me out, like I hadn't known that she was gone before finding her grave, I could have no motive whatsoever for wanting her dead, and I'd never set foot on the hill gardens until a week ago?

In the process of thinking through all this, I realized that I was arguing with myself out loud and could feel my face and eyes contort into an *Angry Birds* embodiment. I resolved to call Augie when I got home, calmed down, and started thinking of more pleasant things.

The sea breeze had started to roll in and I was pondering which bottle of wine to decant when we returned. Was it a Chilean red night? Or more of a Napa Sauvignon type of evening? I was so lost in my oenophile reverie that I nearly ran into a man standing on the sidewalk.

"I'm so sorry," I said and noticed that I was speaking to the one and only Bobby Snyder, Esq.

"Entirely my fault," he quickly corrected. "I just met the nicest family and was still focused on helping them, so I wasn't looking where I was going."

Bardot looked up from her "Facebook page" and did a full sniff workup on the man.

Seeing him close up made him no less slimy. Even the straw derby that you might see a gentleman sporting while punting on the Thames didn't soften his snake oil salesman demeanor.

"I guess we were both distracted," I said, trying to slip past him and put some distance between us.

"What a wonderful dog," he said, crouching down to pet Bardot and therefore yanking my leash arm backward while my body was in full forward motion. I gave Bardot a sneer, but she was not budging. She greeted him with part suspicion and part sneer. I'd have to compliment her good taste with a treat later.

"Allow me to introduce myself, I am Bobby Snyder, Esq.; though I really must drop the suffix, a bit pretentious, don't you think? Do you own one of these marvelous homes around here?"

"Why do you ask?"

I didn't want to divulge any personal information, but I did want to hear his sales pitch. He was practically salivating at having found a new prospect, and with his extra-long neck and curved upper back, he looked like a hungry hyena. The pencil mustache wasn't doing him any favors either.

"I have been visiting with the good people in this neighborhood and offering my services in procuring additional value and income from the very same homes they reside in. How long have you lived here, Miss—?"

"A little over a year. So what services do you provide?"

"Well, I have a booklet of information I'd be

happy to walk you through. Shall we rejoin to your house?"

"Here is fine, I really don't have much time so if you could, just give me the Cliff Notes version."

"I see, perhaps I could drop by at a more convenient time?"

He was really getting eerily persistent in wanting my address. Bardot sensed this and tried to pull me away.

"I'm afraid not," I said, and we started to walk on.

"You do know that oil has been detected almost directly under the sidewalk that you are standing on?"

That stopped me.

"How can you be so sure?" I asked.

"Do you know that with the purchase of your home you also bought the mineral rights?"

"I would have to check, are you able to provide proof that there is oil under here?"

"Absolutely, my dear, I'll show you when we meet. What is your house number?"

"Is this the best way to reach you?" I asked, waving the flyer he had given me while pointing to the phone number at the top.

"It is indeed, would tomorrow work?"

He had now removed his derby and was literally standing with hat in hand. His voice was sounding familiar, but I couldn't place it.

Bardot was warming up her chops for a guttural growl.

"I'll call if I'm interested. Come on, Bardot."

I was in a "take no prisoners" mood. When I got home, I left a message for Augie to call me. Then I called Sally.

* * *

"Cheers," said Peggy, happy to be included in this impromptu mini Wine Club. Sally said that she had picked her up on the way over to my house.

We were all sitting around the end of my pool, dangling our legs in the cool but pleasant water. Bardot had decided to do laps and would periodically check on us to see if any food or toys had been produced. I told them about my day and the discovery of Malcolm's identity. They'd had no idea.

"I have a hard time believing that sweet young Malcolm is a killer," Sally said, holding her glass up to the fading sunlight to note the deep yellow color that told her that this wine had been aged in an oak barrel. "Then again there's nothing about a caterpillar that says it is going to be a butterfly either."

Peggy and I just let that one float.

"I still have some friends at the Agency," Peggy said, referring to her brief stint with the CIA, "let me see what they can pull up on Malcolm and his extended family."

"While you're at it, have them check on that oily lawyer, Snyder." Sally shook her head, trying to cast off the image of him. "That guy gives me the creeps, why are all these real estate vultures suddenly descending on us?"

"That's it!" I declared.

They looked at me, waiting for clarification.

"I thought Bobby Snyder's voice sounded familiar, and now I remember why. He was one of the people in the yelling fest we overheard outside Howard Platz's construction site."

"Well, I'll be darned," Peggy said. "It seems that Rose Avenue is running rampant with people who aren't exactly who they say they are. We might as well be in Beverly Hills!"

Chapter 9

The next morning I had a meeting with my local Coast Guard client at their headquarters in Marina del Rey, the world's largest man-made small boat harbor.

The Marina serves multiple audiences. It is a safe harbor for any vessels in distress, it is home to the yachts of the rich and famous and to the early houseboat settlers who would be hard-pressed to make it out past the jetty.

Along the main channel lies Fisherman's Village, a waterfront mall, a commercial boat anchorage, and a tourist attraction with live music concerts, restaurant and café dining, harbor and fishing cruises, boat and bicycle rentals, a Catalina island ferry service, and a few souvenir shops.

And at the westernmost end is the Coast Guard station. Last year I had built an online secured extranet for their internal communications during search and rescue missions. The data was also encrypted and sent to Homeland Security's internal system. It has worked out well for them and as funding became available, they've been adding more features and depth to the website. This kind of project was right in my wheelhouse, and I'll admit that I was getting used to meeting with cute guys in swim trunks.

What? Jack? I'm not dead, you know.

The most senior member of the station was the exception, having opted for sweats instead. When our meeting ended, I didn't miss an opportunity to ask for a little history lesson. I knew that he had lived here all his life.

"If you have a minute, Captain, I was wondering what these beach areas were like, say fifty years ago or so."

I knew this would get his juices going.

"It gets stuffy in here, let's go outside and sit on the cutter, Halsey. I'll paint you a picture."

I followed him out and onto the Coast Guard boat. I'll admit that I felt more than a little proud as tourists stared and took pictures.

Now if I could just score one of those sweatshirts. . . .

"You'd really have to go back seventy or eighty years to get the full story. I'm old, but I'm not ancient, so much of what I tell you is secondhand from my folks. It all started with tobacco millionaire Abbot Kinney around 1905. He decided to call the area just south of here 'Venice' and set out to turn it into a place with a renaissance of art, culture, and music. He dug canals into the swampland and filled them with gondolas. He built ornate music halls, hotels, and opera houses."

"Wow, I knew about the canals but not about turning the whole area into an Italian resort."

He nodded.

"People flocked here from downtown Los Angeles and all the way from Pasadena. Sure, they enjoyed the old world European sites, but that is not what kept them coming back week after week."

I watched a sea lion that had decided he'd had enough sun slip back off the dock and into the water. With a flop of the tail, he descended out of sight.

"There was money to be made," he continued, "so attractions that could best be described as 'carnie inspired' cropped up all along the beach area, much like you see on the boardwalk today. 'Fun for the whole family,' the barkers would say. There were carnival rides, you could see Chiquita, the world's smallest woman, visit a collection of 'Egyptian' mummies, and even follow the rumors of headhunting cannibals roaming around."

"Today we call those people real estate developers," I quipped.

"By the crash in 1929, no one had the money to spend on roller coaster and miniature train rides. And with Prohibition, people had moved their drinking to less public places. People were desperate for money, and it's said that the first oil was discovered in someone's side yard. Next thing you knew there were three hundred and forty wells on ten acres, pumping day and night."

My ears perked up at this. "So you could be sunbathing on the beach and almost directly behind you up was coming a bubbling crude?"

"Exactly. But greed depleted the oil by the 1940s and everyone pulled out, leaving terribly polluted swampland. That was when this area was cleaned up and began to become residential. Eventually the Marina was built."

"Do you think that there is still oil under the ground around here?"

He chuckled. "Are you thinking that you might be sitting on a fortune under your home, Halsey?"

"Not at all, but we've had a shady sounding lawyer knocking on doors in the neighborhood, offering to secure mineral rights for our properties."

"You're too smart for that. But I will tell you that from time to time over the years rumors crop up of someone finding a trace or so. And of course offshore drilling still goes on up and down this coastline."

He pointed out past the break wall, and I could just make out an oil rig on the horizon.

"Time for our patrol, Cap," said a petty officer from the dock.

"What do you say, Halsey, care to go out on a mission?"

"You won't have to ask me twice," I eagerly replied.

Just when they were getting set to unmoor, my cell phone went off and I saw that it was Marisol. She's a pain in the butt; however, she really doesn't like talking on the phone, so I figured that it must be important.

"What?" I asked, almost hoping that she just had a gossip tidbit that she was dying to tell me.

"Your house was broken into, I called the cops, you better come home."

BARDOT!

I raced up my front steps two at a time.

"Where is she?" I screamed when I entered the house. My eyes wouldn't register anything else until I could spot my dog.

"Right here," I heard Marisol say. "Why'd you lock her in the bathroom?"

"I didn't lock her—Oh, Bardot, are you okay, honey?"

I petted her and hugged and kissed her where she was sitting, with her leash on at Marisol's feet. On cue, she rolled on her back, showed the world her crown jewels, and waited for tummy rubs.

"Well, at least she doesn't appear to be hurt or traumatized," I said.

"You think?" Marisol was enjoying looking down at me.

It was at that point while sitting on the floor that I started to register what had happened. The wicker basket next to one of the sofas that I keep current magazines in had been turned over and it looked like all the periodicals had been fanned through. Cabinets, side tables, anything with drawers or shelves had been ransacked.

"It looks like a cyclone came through here. Are the other rooms like this?" I asked Marisol.

"Wouldn't know, Augie told me to wait at the door and not touch anything until he gets here."

I gave her a hard stare.

"Pretty much," she finally replied. "Are you the one who keeps a pile of clothes at the foot of her bed or did the robber pull them out of your closet and put them there?"

"I hate you."

Suddenly Bardot was on her feet and I feared that the burglar had returned to the scene of the crime.

"Why am I not surprised?" came a voice from behind my back.

Bardot's tail went into mach one rotation with delight.

"You made good time, Augie," Marisol said to him. "Did you take side streets? Because at this time of day school's letting out and traffic is a mess."

Thank you, Air 7 traffic reporter.

"What seems to have happened?" Augie asked, entering my house with a couple of uniforms.

"You're the detective, detect!" I commanded.

"Check for forced entry," Augie told his guys. "Was this door unlocked and open when you came in, Marisol?"

"No, I used the extra key she'd given me. I had to make sure that Bardie was okay."

One: I rue the day I gave her a key. Two: I hate it when she calls my dog "Bardie."

Augie walked around the living room, surveying the damage. He checked some of the magazines on the floor, certainly to make more of a personal judgment on me rather than the perp.

"Crime scene will be here shortly to collect evidence. What can you tell me is missing, Halsey?"

"I really haven't had a chance to look, the obvious things, TVs, the little bit of silver I have, and any big items of value appear to still be here."

"No forced entry from any of the windows in the rooms around the house, Augie." One of the cops informed him.

"What about this back building?" Augie asked me, looking through the glass facing the patio.

"That's my office, and whenever I leave I turn on the alarm, it's wired to the police. If anyone had tried to break in, I would have gotten a call."

Augie nodded and shifted his focus to the big glass doors facing the backyard and pool. He put on a pair of latex gloves and walked over to them.

Crap.

When he tested the door it opened easily.

"There doesn't appear to be a key for these it only locks on the inside. Marisol, did you open the back doors when you got in here?"

"No, Augie, you told me not to touch anything and I didn't."

And I have a bridge that I'm trying to unload. . . .

Augie looked at me.

"I, um, I don't always lock those doors if I'm leaving Bardot home, figured that she would be the best deterrent."

I looked at her and she was on her back again, playing a game of catch with the extra length of leash that Marisol was holding.

"We'll need to wait for the evidence, but it seems likely that someone came by, tried the doors and windows, and when the perp found one open, he came in looking for valuables. He was probably stopped short by Marisol before he could really steal anything."

She beamed.

"So you think that this is random?" I asked.

"You have reason to believe that it isn't?"

"Reasons, several. Bardot is relaxed now but this is her home, and if a stranger broke in, they'd be sorry. Remember what she did to the thieves at the Marina last year."

Augie had to nod as he recollected. Bardot had literally made a drug bust, and I couldn't have been more proud. She'd taken a beautiful leap from the jetty onto a boat of drug smugglers who'd kidnapped me and sent them sprawling to the deck. The Coast Guard then blocked the boat from moving past the breakwater.

"So this had to be someone that Bardot knew and at least tolerated. The feeling appeared to be mutual, otherwise why put her safely in the bathroom? He or she could have kicked her out of the house and left through the front."

"She's got a point, Augie."

He gave Marisol a disgusted, relenting look. I recognized it immediately as it was my standard reaction when she was right.

"So you have a theory?" he asked me.

I filled him in on my encounter with Malcolm, his strange behavior, and the discovery that Abigail Rose was most likely his relative. Augie confirmed this and told me that they were still investigating, but so far everything about the inheritance seemed legit.

"So why is Malcolm keeping this a secret, Augie?"

"Maybe because it's none of your business and he wants to preserve his privacy?"

"Never trust a redhead, they don't tan and they're terrible at hide and seek," Marisol said on her way out of the room.

No words.

I then launched into the Bobby Synder story, and he kind of chuckled at what seemed to him to an obvious con attempt. I explained that Bardot had met both men.

I could see that I was getting nowhere with Augie, and I realized why. I dreaded to admit to him that I had withheld evidence, but I had to tell him about the deed, knowledge of its existence provided a motive. But who wanted it the most?

When I'd finished telling him the details, I gave him a good look to make sure that he hadn't had a stroke. I had watched his neck's jugular vein grow and pulse as I was speaking.

"Who wants a snack?" Marisol asked, coming out of my kitchen with a cheese tray.

WTF????

The uniforms wanted to pounce, but Augie gave them the death stare.

"Just give me the cigar box and all the contents, Halsey, and we are out of here. After I talk to some people at the station, I'll let you know what charges they may want to impose."

"Um, I'm afraid I can't do that," I whispered.

"Why not?" He pretty much screamed.

"Because I don't have them anymore."

True.

"What do you mean you don't have them, where are they?"

Out of the corner of my eye I caught a glimpse of Marisol and Bardot sampling a wedge of my runny Port Salut cheese.

"The deed is with an historian I know being analyzed, the ring is at a museum being appraised, and the tin went along with it."

Half true. I didn't have the deed because I'd hidden it in a safe place after Malcolm's visit.

"I need to leave right now," Augie said.

"Want some wine to go with that cheese?" I said to Marisol.

She stopped chewing just long enough to consider my offer and then shook her head.

Chapter 10

"I'll have the Gulf Stream, dressing on the side, please," Penelope said to the server.

"The Spruce Goose sandwich," Peggy chimed in, "but instead of that whole wheat business can you make it with a nice, warmed roll?"

As the rest of the orders were taken, I admired my surroundings and smiled at the comfort of being with my friends at our favorite local eatery. That just happened to boast a well-represented wine list.

We were having lunch at the Spitfire Grill on the grounds of the Santa Monica airport. The restaurant was opened in the '50s to give the Douglas Aircraft personnel a place to eat in between working on DC-3s, B-17 Flying Fortresses, and the B-47 Stratojet. The walls are filled with WWII military memorabilia, maps, posters, props, and other Douglas Aircraft souvenirs. And it has all the major food groups: bar, flat screen TVs, and booths.

Once we were done with our food selections it was on to the requisite wine choice, though we weren't celebrating anyone's birthday. Brilliant Sally had remarked that we'd gone a week without another murder and that had provided sufficient excuse to imbibe. We chose the medium-bodied Hess Select Chardonnay for its refreshing Monterey fruit forward style.

With glasses filled and condiments on the table for every possible flavor profile, it was time to compare notes in our investigation. I began since I probably had the most news to share and because it might help clarify some of their findings.

"What?" Paula said while loading her veggie burger with, you guessed it, more veggies. "Malcolm is the kindest, most obliging young man I've ever met. He is also very modest, which is probably why he hadn't gotten around to telling us about his great- grandmother. But you know what they say, 'sometimes it's the quiet ones.' "

"It does seem awfully risky and pointless to kill her, after all she was in her nineties and suffering from progressive degenerative brain disease," Sally clinically said. "Time was not on her side."

I continued eating my aquaflight fish tacos while listening to the others theorize. It was good to get some perspective.

"Now that Bobby Snyder is another story entirely," Peggy said.

"Were you able to get more on him from your, um, contacts?" I knew that Peggy liked to keep her past CIA affiliation on the down low.

"Just scratching the surface but if he is a lawyer, there's no record of it with the bar."

"Interesting, and how did he get involved in mineral rights, I wonder?" Penelope had been quiet up until now, not being a fan of Malcolm she'd followed the "if you don't have anything nice to say, say nothing at all" rule.

"That's the key," I said. "Is this just an opportunistic scam that he happened upon or is he working on a bigger scheme?"

"Interesting, go on," Peggy said, starting to catch my drift.

"Well, just suppose that somehow he knew or had heard that a deed could be around out there that gave the bearer mineral rights for the entire area? Maybe he got Howard the developer to float that story about finding oil to try and flush the deed out?"

"You said, and I agree, that it was his voice we overheard during the argument at Howard Platz's property," Sally told the group. "I think that we have to establish a connection between those two men."

"I say we add them to the list but not forget about Malcolm," Penelope said.

Why was Penelope so against Malcolm? From what I could see they'd had minimal contact with each other. Yet she was clearly trying to paint him as a murderer.

"So, I'll keep digging into Malcolm and Snyder's past, and see what else I come up with," Peggy announced.

"And I'm going to apply some serious scrutiny to Mr. Howard Platz. I might go downtown to look up all his property records," Sally decided.

"Great, Penelope you said that you have some initial analysis on the ring that I found?"

"Yes, I'll go over it with you when we're outside," she softly said directly to me. *Odd*.

"Paula, anything more on the possibility of oil being under Rose Avenue?"

"I've gotten a box of Max's papers down from the attic," she said to me. "I have to go through them, but I'm waiting for a time when he is out of the house for a couple of hours."

We all looked at her.

"Seeing anything to do with his study upsets him," she offered as a reason.

"I'm dying to know, what did your appraiser think of the ring?" I asked Penelope.

We'd moved next door to a bench facing the DC-3 "Spirit of Santa Monica" monument in front of the Museum of Flying. Above us, abundant date palms had carpeted the lawn and walkway with their delectable fruit.

"Grace says that it clearly is from the Victorian era, and this is why she needed the ring, she found a hidden latch on the face that opens to a small compartment. It's called a 'poison signet ring' and in those days it held powders that could be slipped into a drink with fatal results to the consumer."

"Wow, they didn't fool around back then. So is Grace sure it is real?"

"Not a hundred percent but not all the metallurgy tests are back," Penelope said, getting up to leave.

"Okay," I said, catching up with her. "May I have the ring back now, I want to see this compartment for myself, and I guess I need to eventually turn it in to Augie for evidence."

"Grace needed to hold onto it for more testing and such," Penelope said, walking quickly away. "Must run, have an appointment. Ta-ta for now, Halsey."

I stopped and watched her disappear up the hill. What was so secret about this discovery that it couldn't be shared with the group, I wondered. Is it because this ring is potentially worth a fortune? And why did the jeweler need to hold onto it, she'd had it for a week.

Something didn't seem right here, or maybe I just needed to stop drinking at lunch. . . .

I spent the afternoon doing a little housekeeping and trying to sort out this mess in my mind. The sooner I can move myself off the suspect list the better.

"Feel like a hot dog and a beer?" Jack asked, coming into the house.

"You spoil me," I said, noticing how cute he looked in a baseball jersey and cap.

"You remember my friend Mark?" he asked,

kissing me. "DEA K-9 team? His son is in Little League and they have a big game tonight. I said I'd watch and cheer him on."

"Whatever will I wear? Seriously, I'm going to have to change. What time do we have to leave?" I asked, heading to my bedroom closet.

This actually sounded like fun, and I needed to be appropriately attired. Meaning Daisy Dukes, sports socks, and Jack Purcells. Was it too much if I wore a baseball shirt too?

"Game starts in about twenty minutes, but don't worry, we're just going up the hill."

"You want me to return to the scene of the crime?? I'm not sure that this is a good idea."

"Why? We'll be on the inland side of the hill, facing away from the gardens. Sitting with all the other parents watching their kids play."

I could tell by his grin that he'd said this just to get a rise out of me. Jack was always trying to steer our relationship into a more serious direction. I was still gun-shy from my divorce and enjoying my freedom. We did this dance more and more often lately.

"I don't think I want to go," I said not liking the Daisy Dukes look.

"Come on, it'll be fun for the whole family. I've got Bardot's leash on and she's very excited."

"She's always excited."

I completely avoided the gardens as we made our way to the top of the hill, making a beeline for the diamond. I figured that if I didn't look over there, then no one would notice me. You could feel the excitement in the air as the players, all suited up, took the field.

Okay, I was having fun, and the kids are super cute. I'd stuck with the Daisy Dukes and that had maybe not been such a good idea because the bleacher seats were metal and cold. I decided not to complain. When Jack told me he'd be right back and then re-appeared with a towel to warm my butt, all was good again in paradise.

"How old are these kids supposed to be?" I asked Jack, watching the pitcher do his wind up.

"Eleven or twelve, why?"

"Because the guy pitching looks like he could drive farm equipment."

"All depends on what you feed them. There's Mark, I'm going to go over and say hi. Back in a minute and I'll bring hot dogs."

"Say hello from me too, and find out which boy is his so we can cheer loudly!"

I watched my gentle giant make his way around the field and jog over to his friend. Jack wasn't what I'd call a deep thinker, but he sure did enjoy life. Where I come from, guys like that get snapped up in a New York minute. Maybe it was time.

Or no.

My mind raced back to the day I realized that my ex-husband, the guy I'd married, was actually a figment of my imagination. The person who emerged from my woolgathering was not the man of my dreams, he was the man of my *bad* dreams.

But Jack was different, wasn't he? I knew the real Jack. I let my mind drift into the reverie of a perfect marriage.

Crap, I'm doing it again.

My thoughts were interrupted by a bit of yelling and commotion coming from behind me at the entrance to the gardens. I couldn't quite make out everything that was being said over the noise of the game and fans, but I did hear this:

"I just wanted to take a look, I'm sorry."

If I didn't immediately recognize the voice, I sure did when I turned and looked at the speaker. It was Malcolm apparently trying to sneak into the gardens by jumping the fence. His hands were raised in a surrender position and I saw him backing away. He had no reason to look in my direction, so I could spy undetected. Something else was said to him and he nodded, turned tail, sped off down the hill.

Now that was interesting.

"Here you go, babe," Jack said, handing me a hot dog. "The one to watch is number five in the blue jersey, his name's Donny."

"We'll have to eat on the way, we've got to check on my garden plot," I said, hopping down from the bench.

My curiosity and Bardot's nose led the way. The police tape was finally gone but the boards they'd used to cover the grave were still a reminder of the horrible discovery. It was hard to tell if anything had been disturbed recently, the whole plot looked like a troop of scouts had marched through it.

"I found dessert," Jack said, showing me a handful of strawberries.

"We're not supposed to take other gardeners' produce; it's a cardinal rule, Jack."

"They were very ripe and needed to be picked. So what's going on, why are we here?"

I explained about Malcolm, Jack had never met him, and about the altercation I had just witnessed when he was trying to jump the fence.

"Why do you think that he was up here trying to sneak into the gardens?"

"Could be a number of things ranging from innocently wanting to visit his great- grandmother's grave to knowing about and wanting to find the deed and the ring. He was trying real hard to sneak looks at my desk and computer screen when he dropped by my office."

"Maybe I should pay him a visit and bring along Clarence to get his take on the Malcolm dude."

Clarence was Jack's giant schnauzer, a large and imposing dog that Jack had so well trained you could take him to tea at the palace.

"Hmm, what would you say to him?"

"Just welcome him to the neighborhood, say I was passing by, walking my dog, and explain my connection to you. And, if Clarence were to accidentally slip his collar and barge into the house, well, I'd have to go in after him. I could throw in a little growling at Malcolm if you'd like?"

"I like the way you think but let's leave out the

growling, I'd like Clarence to give him a true litmus test."

"You got it. So you're really going to plant grapes here?"

"That's the plan, but right now I'd prefer to drink them. Shall we go home?"

"I thought you'd never ask."

Chapter 11

Peggy dropped by on her afternoon walk the next day to say hello and get in some quality petting time with Bardot.

"You are so beautiful, Bardot," she said, snuggling her. Bardot naturally was eating this up.

We were having iced teas out back, and I was loving the fact that daylight was finally getting longer.

"I've got a bit more to add on the research my associate was doing," she started. "It appears that Mr. Bobby Snyder, Esq. is not qualified to use the identifier 'esquire' as part of his formal address."

"What do you mean? He said he was thinking of dropping it, I guess I never really understood what it meant in the first place."

"Well, historically in England it was used to show respect to men of higher social rank. These days it should only be used as a suffix for someone who is a licensed attorney."

Bardot was bored with the direction of the conversation and had opted to roll on the grass on her back in serpentine fashion.

"So Snyder lost his license to practice law?"

"It appears that he never had one, unless it was under a different name."

"So this oil rights offer is just one big scam?"

"It would seem so. Question is, is he working alone?"

"We know we heard his voice in the argument at Howard the developer's construction site. I think that it's time we did an inspection of our own."

"It'll be fully dark by nine. Shall I swing by and pick you and Bardot up?"

"Great, and bring a couple of flashlights if you have them. Should we ask Sally to join us?"

"Nah, let's leave it to all the single ladies."

"Put your hands up," I said to Bardot, and she stood on her hind legs and did just that.

For our mission that night I'd changed into jeans and traded my sandals for Keds sneakers. I even had the common sense not to wear my white ones. I heard footsteps on my front stoop and opened the door for Peggy. Beside her stood Marisol, dressed in black and wearing sneakers over fuzzy, multi-colored, calf-high socks.

"Oh, no, this is not going to work at all," I said to Marisol.

"Are you kidding, it was my idea and I'm going with you."

Peggy gave me a cocked head, questioning look, and I realized that it wasn't worth trying to explain. It was Marisol who had made a suggestion of going at night when I returned from our first visit to the construction site.

"Can I borrow one of those flashlights?" Marisol asked me as I locked the door.

"No! If you're going to crash our recon, then you're going to have to do it in the dark. How did you know that we'd planned to go tonight anyway?"

"She must have seen me crossing over to your house, Halsey."

I looked at Marisol for confirmation and saw that her face was blank.

"Possibly," I said not buying it for an instant. She'd been dressed for a B and E. "But more likely she's bugged my place and knew what we were planning."

"Did not! Are we going to stand here or are we going on our mission?"

"Our mission?"

Bardot seemed to agree with Marisol and was pulling me down the street.

At this time of night Rose Avenue was really magical. The huge Chinese elm and bottlebrush trees that lined the street swayed gently in the ocean wind. Soft lighting shone on porches and front doors often broadcasting the season with appropriate wreaths or flags. In many yards, kids' toys lay dropped in place when bedtime curfew rang.

"So what's the plan?" Peggy asked, bringing me back to the task at hand.

"Well, I downloaded a special camera app so

that I can take photos in very low light. I figured that we should do a perimeter search and work our way to the middle, looking for anything that seems odd or telling."

"I'm going to be looking for cigarette butts," Marisol proclaimed.

"What? Why on earth?" Peggy really didn't speak "Marisol."

"It'll keep her out of our hair," I whispered to Peggy.

"I heard that."

We turned the corner of Rose and could just make out the construction site by the moonlight. Bardot had gone into hunting and tracking mode, something that Jack had trained her to do when he took her on practice rescue missions for CARA. Basically he'd let her smell an article of clothing from a missing person and she'd use that to complete the rescue. In the event that a family member or friend couldn't provide an item with the victim's scent, he would have the dog follow a scent picked up at the victim's last known whereabouts through dead ends and leads until they finally tracked down and rescued the person.

I'd practiced this on drills with Bardot but somehow we'd always get sidetracked and start playing. I'd always hoped that in a real emergency she and I'd respect the seriousness of the situation and pull off the rescue.

Tonight, even though she was walking with friends in her own neighborhood Bardot seemed to recognize that this was business, and she walked low to the ground focused primarily on scents.

Several dogs from the houses we passed barked but Bardot paid absolutely no attention.

When we reached the gate in the fence, we saw that a heavy chain secured the gate shut to the neighboring metal post. The padlock that held the chain together looked like one of those from the ads where they shoot at it and the bullet bounces off, demonstrating indestructibility. Peggy and I looked at each other weighing our options.

"Over here," Marisol called to us from around the side.

I turned on a flashlight and we followed the sound of her voice. The property line backed up carefully manicured tall shrubbery that concealed a parking lot that was part of the Santa Monica airport. It was used to handle the heavy crowds that sometimes came to a giant hangar to see award shows, concerts and galas, and outlet clothing sales. In other words, there'd be no one there tonight to hear us prowling around.

When we found Marisol, she was crouching at the very end of the fence that met the concrete wall of the parking lot. She seemed to have worked the bottom corner of the chain-link fencing up and away from the wall. There was an opening of about one and a half feet around. I looked around for bolt cutters or something else she must have used to pry this open.

"How did you do this, it was you, right?" I looked at her and saw the gold-toothed grin.

"I'm impressed," Peggy said, "but surely you had help?"

"Nope, but I've been working on it for a few

days now. Once I got a little bit peeled back, then I could work on it easier with a heavy-duty pry bar."

"Where the hell did you get that?" I asked.

"Borrowed it from one of the workmen."

"Did he ask why you needed such a robust tool?" Peggy was finally starting to speak a little "Marisol."

"Told him that I needed to take down a shelf in the garage, I also brought him some cheese enchiladas. He didn't ask any more questions."

"How come you never bring me enchiladas?" I knew that I was walking right into it.

"Don't need anything from you, that's why."

"Shall we, ladies," Peggy suggested. "I'm not getting any younger."

Once we squeezed through, we were amazed at how little had really been accomplished.

"How long would you say that they've been at this?" I asked Peggy.

"At least two, maybe three months. I've got no clue what they've been doing behind this fenced curtain, all I see is mud, garbage, and some really crude framing of only a part of the house."

"I wonder where this famous basement is going to be dug," I said, taking in the small views of the site from the light of my flashlight.

I saw Marisol disappear into the center wooden structure and let Bardot off her leash. I knew she'd keep Marisol from danger.

"Did you ever see the movie *The Producers*?" Peggy asked me.

"Hilarious, I remember that. Weren't they putting on a ridiculous play titled, *Springtime for Hitler*?"

"That's the one. Max Bialystock was a washed-up Broadway producer who seduces elderly women in return for investing in his shows. When his accountant, the fabulous Gene Wilder, comes in to do his books, he discovers the money. The two join forces, knowing that they can make much more money if a play is a flop. If it is so bad that it closes after one performance, then they don't have to pay back the investment money."

"Right, I remember, and they build a totally putrid show that is a runaway hit foiling their get rich quick scheme. So what are you thinking here, that Howard the developer is delaying progress to file an insurance claim?"

"I don't know exactly how those things work, but yes. Or he could be stalling in the hopes that he strikes oil and then will never have to finish the damn thing. He told us he had the mineral rights to that property and seemed to pooh-pooh their value. But perhaps he's another one on the hunt for that deed."

Peggy really did know how to think like a criminal. Residue from her CIA days I suspect. Just then, I heard a series of barks from Bardot.

"I've got to quiet her down and check on Marisol," I said and ran to the wood framing. The closer I got the muddier the soil got, sucking hard on my shoes with each step. For a split second I thought about the oil that may be beneath the surface. As I entered the structure, it got very dark and I turned on my flashlight. Bardot was standing at the far end, her head down and whining. It was the same sound she'd made when she dug up Abigail Rose in the garden.

"Bardot, stay," I commanded in a loud whisper. "I'm coming."

I started running again, praying that I would not find Marisol injured and on the ground. And, of course, the batteries were dying in my flashlight. I took a big step forward and this time the earth successfully claimed my left shoe, sending me facedown in the mud and propelling me forward. The last thing I remember is the ground disappearing beneath me and then feeling a heavy, dull pain on my chest.

I felt something cold moving around my face and I opened my eyes. Big mistake. Whoever was the first to use "Here's mud in your eye!" as a drinking toast had clearly never actually had mud in their eye. I turned over on my back and felt for a dry patch of sleeve to clean my face. This time I felt something warm, breath in and out next to my ear, and realized that it was Bardot. When I looked up, I was blinded by the aura of a bright light that had suddenly been turned on.

"What are you two doing down there?"

Marisol. Of course.

"I thought I was coming to rescue you. Could you please shine that light away from my eyes?"

"Your face don't look so good," Marisol said, redirecting the beam.

"Oh dear, Halsey," Peggy said. "Why would you go into this trench?"

"Why does everybody think that I ended up here on purpose?"

"Are you alright, should I call 9-1-1?"

"I'm fine, Peggy, I just had the wind knocked out of me. But can you toss me down a flashlight? Also I'm looking at my phone and I don't have any bars. I know it gets reception on the sidewalk. We need to find a way for me to send it up to you so you can call Jack. Hopefully we can still make it out of here unnoticed."

I picked up the flashlight Peggy had tossed and checked my immediate surroundings. I was standing in about two inches of water, and when I put some on fingers and looked closer, it was mixed with some black sludge. I took a whiff and could detect sulfur. Not pleasant.

"How's this?" I heard and shone the light up. Marisol had a length of rope and tied to the end of it was something white with an odd shaped cup.

"That should work if the rope's long enough. Send her down."

While I waited, I realized that Bardot was nowhere to be seen. At the very least, she was out of flashlight range. I called for her.

I felt the rope land on my shoulder and swung around to catch it. I pulled my phone out of my pocket and in doing so tripped on the backlight of my home screen, illuminating the white pouch attached to the rope.

"Is this a bra?" I shouted. "Yours, Marisol?"

"Of course, what'd you think; this place isn't Vicky's Secret."

"Good one," Peggy said, laughing.

"Disgusting," I said, securing the phone in her size 34 B cup, "you can pull the rope up now."

A moment later we all froze as Bardot let out a high-pitched, plaintive wail.

"BARDOT!"

I ran toward her while tapping my flashlight on my thigh to get the last bit of juice out of the batteries.

"Yikes!" I screamed in horror.

If you've ever seen a dog's eyes catching light in otherwise total darkness, then you know that it is not a pretty sight. Bardot's glowed a demonic green, making me think that she'd been possessed by a very evil Kermit the Frog. When I could make out the floppy ears, I calmed down a bit.

"You guys okay?" Peggy called down, shining the light from my phone.

I knew what I was going to find even before I saw it. Bardot had made that sound only once before. Then I caught sight of work boots attached to a big lifeless body.

"Peggy? Now would be a really good time to call Jack . . ."

Chapter 12

The partially covered structure of the framed area provided only minuscule insulation from the cold night air. Jack had pulled me out of the wet ditch, but my sneakers were soaked through, and I was pretty sure that I was harboring a pound of mud under my shirt.

"Where do you think you're going?" I asked Marisol, tugging her back by her sleeve.

"Home. This party's over."

"Oh no you don't, you're as much a part of this as the rest of us. You are going to wait for Augie and then you are going to tell him exactly what happened. And how the killer could have been any one of us who found the body."

"Here, Marisol," Jack said, bringing in a plastic chair from outside our refuge. She took a seat, beaming at the attention and respect.

"You sure you're not hurt?" he asked me tenderly.

"I'll let you know after Augie has been and gone."

"You did nothing wrong, honey, but we'll need to explain away what we were doing here in the first place," Peggy said, always thinking ahead.

"We'll say that we ran in after Bardot. Marisol, give Peggy your chair, she's the one who's eighty-seven!"

"Why?"

"I'll find another one," Jack said as we heard sirens approaching.

It was going on eleven p.m. and the dampness of the site had seeped into my bones. Like Marisol, all I wanted to do was shower and get under the covers with Bardot and Jack, not necessarily in that order. The police cars triggered lights in the neighboring homes, and it wouldn't be long before people came out to see what all the fuss was about.

Twenty minutes later work lamps on stands lit up the space, making it no less eerie. The body of the man was facing away from us on his side, but what I could see of his face looked like the same guy who had stormed out during the argument we'd overheard on our first recon mission.

"Thank you, Auntie," I heard Augie say to Marisol. "I'll have one of the officers drive you home right away."

Who died and made her queen?

"I'm going to talk to Peggy next and then I will get to you, Halsey."

"I can't wait."

Sweet Jack had brought a folding chair from his truck for me, and he and Bardot were crouched beside me. He'd even given me his jacket to throw over my shoulders. I really need to think seriously about keeping him.

"You know, that's two bodies in less than a month," Jack whispered to me.

"Don't remind me, I'm sure that I'll be getting an earful from Augie."

"Not you, Bardot. That's two bodies that *she's* found."

"So?"

The team from the ME's office arrived and immediately took over the scene. We were sitting in a far corner, so they left us alone.

"So, that means that Bardot has the makings of an amazing cadaver dog," Jack continued, petting her.

"I'm afraid to ask . . ."

"A cadaver dog is trained to recover human remains; they're able to locate body parts, blood, any kind of decomposition. CARA is always in need of dogs with those skills."

"EW! I kiss that nose, no thank you."

"Just saying, Bardot is a pooch of many talents."

We watched Augie strut his way over to us, his eyes never leaving mine.

"And now we come to Miss Halsey," Augie said smugly.

"Are you also sticking with the story that you all followed your dog onto the construction site?" Augie asked me.

"Of course, because it's true."

I would have loved to have let him know that dear, sweet Auntie Marisol had been working on getting that fence open for about a week, but it wouldn't have helped with my cause.

"And you just happened to run into my aunt and Mrs. Peggy while taking a late evening walk?"

"Your aunt likes to spy on me and insisted on tagging along. Peggy and I had arranged earlier to meet now that the nights are getting warmer."

That shut him up, temporarily. We all watched as the body was raised from the ditch, and Augie stopped them once it was up so that I could take a shot at identifying him. His skin looked waxy and his face was contorted in a way that made it look like he'd died in mid choke. My stomach churned and I thought that I was going to be sick.

"I only saw him for a minute that day, Augie, it might be the same guy from the argument with Howard, but I can't be sure. In either case, he's the one you should be interrogating, not me."

"We have a unit picking him up now and taking him to the station. While it does seem that you and your friends stumbled in on this, don't think that I believe your story about how you got in here for one minute. I'll be watching you very closely."

"Thanks, Augie, somehow I feel so much safer."

As we headed out to the gate in the fence, I noticed a jacket hanging on a peg of the wood frame that looked about Howard's size. Behind it hung something made of straw.

"We got the results back from Abigail Rose's autopsy report," Augie said, getting my undivided attention.

"And?"

"Asphyxiation. She died by asphyxiation, smothered by the dirt of her grave."

"She was buried alive?"

Before I got my answer I fainted and kissed dirt for the second time that night.

I woke up to breakfast in bed.

"Now this is more like it," I said to Jack, accepting a tray of goodies. On it I saw and smelled the aroma of warm biscuits cradling melting butter, some peach jam, and a perfectly soft-boiled egg. Orange juice that I know was fresh squeezed completed the excellent repast. Bardot sat obediently by the side of the bed.

"Nothing but the best for my sweetie," he said, and I almost didn't mind the corny term of endearment.

"You're dressed and you've got keys in your hand," I said, giving Jack a good look over.

"Afraid so, I have a training session in Malibu in less than an hour."

"Boo!"

"You sure you're feeling okay? I could have Marisol come over."

"God no!"

"Alright," Jack said, chuckling. "Got to boogie." I got a kiss on the cheek.

As soon as I heard the front door shut, Bardot

was up on the bed. She must have been sitting in a springed crouch the entire time.

I kept a laptop in my bedroom, I know, really bad habit. But today it happened to be a good idea because I could catch up on things while having breakfast.

I skimmed through my emails until I came across one from Aimee. I remembered that I'd asked her that, if she had the time during shifts at her yogurt shop, could she do some online research on the history of Mar Vista. I was excited to see what she'd found out.

> Hi!
> I really, really miss you guys, but I am also learning so much in baking class! Yesterday Chef said that I made the best "Ile Flottante" she'd tasted in a long while!
> Anyhoo, I didn't want to let you down on your case and I think I found something that you'll find interesting. It is a draft of a paper that Paula's husband Max had written and I guess he shared it with the guy who has it in an online archive. Don't ask what search steps I took to find it, about halfway through the girls' softball team came in from practice and each one had a special order.
> The paper's attached; I'll try to get back to this when I can. Hugs and kisses to all the girls and a special one to Bardot!
> Aimee

Nice. As I started reading the PDF, I realized that this was going to take all my concentration. I put the depleted tray on the floor, let Bardot in under the covers, and went to work. An hour later, I was still reading.

Chapter 13

"Would you pass the edamame, please?"

I handed the dish of steamed soybeans drizzled with salt and sesame oil down the table to Penelope. Sally and Peggy were discussing the merits of fish-and-chips over crab cakes. By this time they had shared various versions of last night's escapades.

We were having lunch at Tony P's overlooking the Marina; I'd called an emergency meeting after I finished reading the files Aimee had sent me. I wasn't quite sure how to process this new information and was anxious to hear what the group had to say. I'd left Paula out on purpose because I didn't want her opinion clouding what her husband Max had written. Plus, she's a little odd, especially when food is involved.

She's vegan unless baby back ribs are being served. Or steak. A filet, to be exact. She does eat every sort of vegetable, but don't try and tempt her with tofu, regardless of how it's prepared. She calls it the "devil's discard." And Paula I suspect has never been on the fence in her life. She either likes things or abhors them.

As soon as I'd ordered my Creole steamed mussels, I began.

"Max's paper is a detailed chronological history of Mar Vista and particularly the hill. According to Max, it seems that people have been speculating about the grounds where the community gardens and the surrounding neighborhoods sit long past the oil rush of the thirties. Numerous attempts have been made as close as ten years ago to locate a source and tap it. This paper Max was working on was written sometime in 2014, but I have no idea how long ago he started his research," I explained.

"So do you think that people are still trying to find oil up there?" Sally asked, dipping a chip in malt vinegar.

"I haven't seen any evidence of that, but it doesn't mean it doesn't exist," I replied. "Also let's not forget this sudden interest people and developers have with putting in basements. What I fell into at the construction site was not just mud. It had a sulfur-like smell and a gooey consistency."

"So what would happen if they found oil?" Penelope asked. "Would oil derricks be popping up like mushrooms after a good rain?"

"First of all we haven't had a good rain in over three hundred days," Peggy said, "and secondly the real rush would be from the greedy ones who would beg, borrow, steal, and kill for the mineral rights."

"Bingo, that would explain why Mr. Bobby Snyder, Esq. is suddenly a fixture on Rose Avenue."

I looked at Sally, she had a point but this wasn't making things clearer, quite the opposite. And I hadn't dropped the real bomb yet.

"Well, be prepared to have your socks blown off," I said, grabbing their undivided attention. "What I'm about to read to you was in the very last section of Max's report. It almost seems as if he stopped writing in mid-sentence."

I grabbed my iPad from my bag and took a healthy sip of iced tea. We hadn't really considered ordering wine because we all had things to do after lunch, but once they hear this, minds may be changed.

"Some of this passage is quoted directly from the *Herald-Express,* a daily newspaper back then. Here was the headline: 'Werewolf Strikes Again! Kills L.A. Woman, Writes B.D. on Body.' I looked it up and apparently this happened soon after the 'Black Dahlia' murder."

"This is all true? Not something Max had made up?" Sally asked, and I nodded.

"Here's the kicker," I said, and continued reading.

The victim of the "Werewolf Killer" was forty-five-year-old Jeanne French. Her nude body had been discovered at about eight a.m. on February 10, 1947 near Grand View Avenue and Indianapolis Street.

"This is pretty much center of where the baseball field is now," I explained. "The body had been hidden under a pile of weeds."

French had been savagely beaten, and her body was covered with bruises. She had suffered some blows to her head, probably administered by a metal blunt instrument—maybe a socket wrench. As bad as they were, the blows to her head had not been fatal. Jeanne died from hemorrhage and shock due to fractured ribs and multiple injuries caused by stomping—she had heel prints on her chest. It took a long time for French to die.

Jeanne's estranged husband, Frank, was brought in on suspicion of murder. He was later cleared—

"The murder remains unsolved."

Everyone took a breath and let this sink in. Suddenly no one was hungry. We watched a sailboat back out of its berth and maneuver into the main channel.

"One more thing," I said.

"Sweet mother of triplets," Sally swore.

"Last night as we were leaving the construction site, Augie told me that Abigail Rose's autopsy report had come back. It said that she died of asphyxiation, smothered by the dirt of her grave. She was buried alive."

* * *

"So they never found the 'Werewolf Killer.' You don't think that Max had anything to do with this, he couldn't have been more than a little shaver back in 1947," Penelope summed up.

Peggy did the smart thing next and asked the waiter for a wine list.

"Agreed, and there may be no connection between this and Abigail's murder," I said. "But two dead bodies buried in the same area, what are the chances of that? Maybe Abigail's murder was some sort of copycat slaying."

"I wonder why Max stopped writing about this," Sally asked. "Max is meticulous about facts and details; he would never give up on a story."

"I'd say we could just ask Max or Paula about it, but that could just raise false suspicions or look like we are spying on him." I stopped trying to read the dessert menu; I was having fruit, fermented fruit.

"Which is exactly what we *are* doing. Didn't Paula say that she was going to pull some of his research together and give it to us?"

I nodded to Peggy.

"Well, when we get them, we can compare notes. See if he'd added more at a later date."

"This could explain why Paula said that Max doesn't want to talk about the study," Peggy threw into the mix. "And if he was too young to have committed the first murder, maybe that's where he got the idea of how to dispose of Abigail Rose?"

"But why would he need to get rid of the poor dear?" Penelope asked.

"Well, with all his research, he must have a pretty good idea if there's oil to be found around us," Sally replied. "And remember Paula told us that they owned the mineral rights under their property. Maybe Max came upon the trail of the deed. If you recall when he and Malcolm gave us their history lesson, Max ended by saying that he knew there was oil here because he'd seen it."

"Let's not forget about our friend Bobby Snyder. If somehow he knew about the existence of the deed, I'm guessing that he would do just about anything to get his hands on it," Penelope concluded.

"Great, so the murderer could be Bobby Snyder, Malcolm, Howard the developer, Paula's husband Max, or none of the above. I hate it when they do this in books, and I like it even less when it happens in real life," I said.

The next two days were spent working on some additions to the Coast Guard's website; I actually welcomed the break from the murder case. By the third day of coding, my brain hurt. I needed a distraction and Bardot and Jack were just the ones to provide it. We decided that we'd go on a beach run and romp early Saturday morning. Since summer hadn't officially started, we figured that we'd have the place to ourselves and settled on the Venice sand just north of Marina del Rey. Jack brought his giant schnauzer, Clarence, the perfectly trained dog whose manners Bardot could unravel in under a minute.

After about an hour the sun started to rise behind us, the dogs were wet and sandy and Jack and I were in need of food and caffeine. It was times like these when the beach is truly magical. As we sat on the cool sand and watched the waves, sounds of gulls and pelicans coming to life filled the air. The rich, briny smell of the sea got me thinking about oysters and scrambled eggs.

Less than an hour from now the boardwalk behind us would be transformed into the wacky carnival that tourists flock to year around. They will be able to get their fill of henna tattoos, watch a fearless man juggle running chainsaws, and listen to live music ranging from reggae to folk to beat-boxing. But for now as we headed toward sustenance, the only activity came from merchants rolling up metal doors to their stalls and moving out stands displaying their wares. I saw a rather weathered woman pulling out a tall revolving postcard rack and one of the pictures caught my eye.

It was a black-and-white photo of what looked like hundreds of oil wells on the beach just steps away from the shoreline in Venice Beach. When I turned the card over, the caption told me that this photo was taken in 1952. Smoke was billowing out of smaller buildings next to each well that must be driving the pumping. Jack looked at the image over my shoulder and then nodded his head slightly to the owner of the stall.

"Excuse me," he started politely.

She had her back to us. "Not open yet. Come back in about an hour."

"Of course; here, let me help you with that,"

Jack said and lifted another postcard stand directly in the air and waited for her to tell him where she wanted it.

"Just there will do," she said, finally looking at our smiling faces.

"We don't want to disturb your set up; we—I just had a question about the photo on this postcard. We'll come back later. May I get you a coffee or something?" I asked.

She took the postcard I was holding and gave it a long study. "Questions I always have time for, 'specially when it comes to the history of Venice. Most of the tourists these days only want to know if I've seen any of the Kardashians around, or some ask where they can score some weed. Like I would know." She laughed.

I think you would.

"What was it that you wanted to know about this?"

"I've heard stories about people striking oil around here and was wondering how true they were and how long they've kept drilling," I asked, treading lightly. She hid her hefty body under a caftan and her gray hair ran free. Her timeworn face told me that she could be anywhere from fifty to eighty.

"Aw hell, I know people today that swear they are one or two digs away from being rich. But this kind of stuff"—she pointed back to the postcard—"that stopped sometime in the nineties. The oil company gave the city about a half a million to clean up the beach but that didn't even scratch the surface of the damage they'd done. Organizations like Heal the Bay do what they can but rely on volunteers and donations."

"How long have you been working around here, Miss—?"

"Call me Sophie, handsome. And I appreciate the 'miss' part, but I could have taken this photo," she replied.

"Nice to meet you, Sophie, I'm Halsey and this is Jack."

The dogs, realizing that we were going to be here a while, had opted for a nap.

"Well, if you're thinking about drilling for oil, just make sure that you've got all your t's crossed and your i's dotted."

"What do you mean?" I asked.

"Mineral rights, legal stuff. Deeds are king when it comes to oil."

"Thank you, but we're just curious about the history, that's all. I know you're getting ready to open, I'll buy this card and we'll let you get back to it."

"Keep it, the postcard's on me, but since you offered to get me something to drink, I'll take a tall one. Cold this morning, I need something to take the edge off," she said to Jack, as if he'd understand better than I would.

"You got it," Jack said, running off.

Is that what he means when he says "breakfast of champions"?

Chapter 14

"What do you think Sophie's story is?" I asked Jack over my eggs ranchero at Maxwell's.

"Hmm, good question. Let me think for a minute." Which translated meant, *I'm going to enjoy my banana walnut pancakes, eggs, and sausage a while longer before I talk.*

If we ran out of things to talk about, which was seldom, Jack and I loved to play a game that I call "scenario, please?" The way it worked is that you picked a person or couple wherever you are and challenged each other to come up with their story. Once one of us was done, the other could agree, elaborate, or change the story entirely. It was great for getting through airport flight delays and just fun in general.

"I'd say that Sophie is an old soul, and I don't mean because her skin is like leather," Jack finally began. "She's like a 'house mother' to the Venice boardwalk sellers and performers, and I wouldn't be surprised if she carries a deck of Tarot cards on her at all times."

Damn, he's good.

"I'd say that she's been married two or three times, but the last ended over ten years ago even though they never bothered to get a divorce." With that Jack began the thorough process of wiping his carefully cropped beard. He was a bit of a fanatic about having a clean, soft beard, which I greatly appreciated.

"Your turn," he challenged me.

"I'm impressed, but you had to look past the loose dress to recognize that she had once been a crowd-gathering contortionist on the very same sidewalk where she now sells souvenirs. I wouldn't be surprised if she's got a postcard or two with a photo of her in a pretzel-shaped pose from back in the day."

"I should never go first, you can always add a zinger that I could never think of," he said, applauding.

My cell phone rang and I saw that it was Augie.

"If it isn't my favorite public servant," I said into my phone.

"And hello to my most persistent suspect," he answered back. "I wanted to bring you up to date; I've got good news and bad news."

"Great," I said as Jack paid our bill, and we stepped outside so I could put the call on speaker.

"We gave Howard the developer a thorough questioning and in the end let him go."

"Is that the good news or the bad news?" I asked.

"Well, it's good for him and bad for you."

"Come on Augie, we've been all through this and you know I had nothing to do with that poor guy's demise. What did you find out about him anyway?"

"His name was Carlos, Howard was about to fire him, the guy's an angry drunk who also had a drug problem. It seems his wife left him and he never got over it."

"Maybe if he'd cleaned up his little problems . . ."

"Yeah, well, he's had a string of arrests, DUI. He was driving with a suspended license."

"And how do you know that Howard didn't kill him, maybe the firing didn't go so well?"

"Because Howard was at a hockey game, courtesy of the lumberyard he does a lot of business with. It all checked out."

"So who killed Carlos and what was he doing at the site so late at night?"

"I was about to ask you that, Halsey."

"Very funny."

"We'll need the autopsy report to determine cause of death and that should help tell us where to go next. Also we need CSI's report. Rumor has it that they found a couple gallon tanks of gasoline on the premises."

"So maybe Carlos was about to carry out a grudge," Jack said, and I nodded.

"But what or who stopped him?" I added.

"One other thing, has Aunt Marisol talked to you about the DNA test?"

"Is she pregnant again?" I asked, and Jack laughed. Augie did not.

"We got some interesting results on the test

from the cigarette butt that this Bobby Snyder dropped. You know, the lawyer that's trying to sell you all brokered mineral rights packages?"

"I know," I said, thinking about what Sophie had just told me about "legal stuff."

"It seems that his real name is Robert W. Snopes."

"That's why we couldn't find any record of his law license," I said aloud.

"He had one, if passing the bar in South Dakota the easiest test state counts. Records since he started practicing show that he's basically a low-life ambulance chaser."

"You said 'had one,' has he been disbarred?"

"Yes," Augie told me. "He went down in style, having been caught stealing prescription pads from several doctors in a medical group. It seems that he was falsifying diagnoses for his clients in order to up claims on their accident and injury suits."

"So why isn't he serving time and providing legal advice to the fine citizens of federal prison?"

"You've met him, he's a slimy one. He managed to worm his way into a significantly reduced sentence and parole, thanks to hefty bribes no doubt. But as far as the ABA was concerned, 'stick a fork in him, he's done.'"

"You've got to stop him, Augie, before he fools some nice old lady into giving him her life savings."

"Believe me I stressed that to Auntie Marisol."

"I said 'nice old lady,' Augie."

"We'll need something concrete in order to

bring him in for questioning," he said, ignoring my comment once again.

"We're working on it," I told him.

"Oh no you don't, you and your band of winos need to stick to what you do best."

"Which is what, Augie?"

"I haven't figured that out yet."

I spent the next couple of days hunkered down to the work that actually paid the bills. I got a web upgrade proposal off to my Coast Guard client, filled out a questionnaire for a possible new gig with the Santa Monica airport, and did things I'd been neglecting for good reason. Like getting my teeth cleaned, getting Bardot's teeth cleaned, pulling out the patio furniture now that summer was on its way, and paring down Bardot's pool toys from last year that were ratty and ready for retirement. I had to sneak out one night to toss "ducky," a well-worn favorite, while she was asleep. She didn't need to experience the trauma.

I was at my computer early the next morning, enjoying that fresh, clean, and light feeling you get after having completed a necessary evil when Sally walked into the office.

"Nine hundred ninety-nine, one thousand," she declared, confirming the count on her fitness monitor.

"If you've come in here to prod me to exercise more, I will have you know that I've accomplished a great deal this week and am reveling in the glow of progress."

"Actually, I was coming by to see if you wanted to go up to the gardens this afternoon to help Paula harvest her crops. Peggy's bringing a nice chilled King Estate Oregon Pinot Gris."

"Are we driving up there and back?"

"Yes."

"I'm in, and I'll throw something together in the cheese/fat/carb food group to accompany the wine."

"Perfect."

I was relieved to see that the gardens were fairly quiet and that there was no sign of Malcolm. Paula had led the way to her plots, or should I say her "horticultural fiefdom"? They clearly stood out as the Emerald City among the more organic and free-range gardens that were haphazardly doing their thing.

We'd toted along stacks of small crates to transport Paula's bounty and settled ourselves along the perimeter of her first plot that was producing asparagus, carrots, and fava beans. While Peggy worked the corkscrew and Sally readied the wineglasses, I watched Paula whisper something to each carrot before she pulled it up from the ground. She stopped after the second one and seemed to be going through some mental anguish. I'd hoped that this wasn't some sort of *Sophie's Choice* situation, but she did leave one in its place to grow another day.

"Have you lived here all your life, Paula?" I asked,

hoping to interrupt her malaise and worm my way into finding out more about her and her husband.

She nodded, which got me exactly nothing.

"Is this where you and Max met?" I asked, nodding to the gardens.

This time she shook her head.

"Paula's story about finding Max is a good one," Peggy said, urging her on.

Sally passed around filled glasses, and I took the wrapping off a tray of bacon-wrapped figs stuffed with bleu cheese and panko.

Oh, I can deliver.

"Well." She seemed a little flustered having the spotlight swung her way. She took a good sip of wine and settled in to tell her story.

"It was 1968, right around here at the Venice Beach Rock Festival. I was braless, spirited, and twenty-one," she said dreamily. "I remember how excited I was because Janis Joplin was going to appear. It was a psychedelic time, we were hippies, had gurus, soul, and believed in free love."

Who are you and what have you done with Paula?

"Wow," I said, trying to recover from this revelation. "And Max was there?" I was hoping to move her as quickly as possible off of the "free love" part of the story. This was an amazing about-face from the Paula I knew, but we were bordering on TMI.

"The beach was wall to wall people. I was there with my housemates," she continued. Looking to the sky to help her recollect, she listed them: "Begonia, Nico, Tranquilla, Honey, Kyle, Dylan, and Buzz."

"There were eight of you? Must have been a huge house," Sally said.

"Not at all, just three rooms and a small kitchen with a hot plate. We laid out mattresses and futons on almost every bit of floor space. We shared everything and everyone."

"Tell me about the rock festival," I implored. I needed to quash any brewing mental images of Paula during her "experimental" period.

"Well, you couldn't see much of the beach as hundreds of people had lain down to form a giant peace sign. While most of the country was digging out of snow, we were smoking the wacky tabacky and grooving to reggae."

For about a minute she stopped talking, and from the way her upper body was swaying, I knew she was listening to Bob Marley in her head.

"Just outside Muscle Beach, where Schwarzenegger was pumping iron in hopes of becoming Mr. Universe, was a three-guy combo playing Thelonious Monk. A drummer, a keyboardist, and this tall drink of water on the sax."

"Enter Max," I said, pouring her more wine. We were getting to the good part.

"He had on a straw porkpie hat and such a peaceful, eyes-closed expression on his face as he made that saxophone purr. I sat down cross-legged to listen, after a while my friends got bored and moved on."

"Wait, what were you wearing?" I needed to paint the whole scenario in my head.

"Umm, let's see. It was an unseasonably warm day, so next to nothing. A sheer knee-length spaghetti strap white dress. I remember I was the last to get up that morning so no one was there to help me zip up the back. I just left it open."

I suddenly looked at Paula in a totally different way. It may well be that we become caricatures of ourselves in our golden years, but I was seeing a young, hip, beautiful woman falling in love.

"After a long time of staring at him play while his eyes remained closed, I sadly got up to leave. I figured this was a lost cause."

"Oh, Paula," Peggy said, emotional even though she knew that a happy ending was nigh.

" 'Where're you goin'?' he asked me in a silky voice. That's how I met Max. I never did get to see Janis Joplin."

I took a deep breath and smiled. Nothing that romantic has ever happened to me, unless you count a college boyfriend who searched high and low for me at a party just so he could throw up in my hands.

"What are we harvesting next?" Sally asked after we'd all thought about her story for a while. "These look ready," she said, yanking on a handful of onion stalks.

"NO! You can't just pull them out of their beds like that! How would you feel?" Paula asked. She had tears in her eyes and she was starting to hyperventilate.

"I'm sorry, I was just trying to help," Sally said clearly startled by Paula's response. We looked at each other and then at Peggy, all three of us not sure if Paula was having some kind of episode.

"You are such a natural at gardening, Paula," I

said, watching her gently replant each onion. "I was wondering if you wouldn't mind taking a look at my plot, maybe give me some pointers?"

Sally smiled and nodded, thinking that I'd provided a good distraction for Paula.

"What? No. In fact I have to go, right now," she said, grabbing the few crates she'd filled with vegetables. She quickly stormed off, and we watched her disappear down the hill.

"I got nothing," Peggy said.

"She really needs to start wearing a hat when she's out here working in the hot sun," Sally said. "Or she's going to end up planting imaginary seeds in a garden with rubber walls."

Chapter 15

Peggy had Wine Club this week and as much as I love her, I still found it difficult to go to her house. Oh, don't get me wrong, her house is warm and cozy and so clean that even the five-*minute* rule doesn't apply. I know because I once spilled a dish of Jordan almonds on her powder-blue carpet and managed to scoop them up before anyone noticed. And no one was the worse for wear after eating them.

As I alluded to earlier, my discomfort is because the first Wine Club I ever attended was also held at Peggy's. I'd walked into a house with an open door and walked straight through to the back garden where I assumed everyone had gathered. Instead, I found a woman named Rosa lying facedown in the grass with a knife sticking out of her back. It was the first murder recorded for Rose Avenue since, well, since they started counting. And here I am just over a year later at the heart of another murder in the neighborhood. Essentially I'm the "Murder Whisperer."

Peggy was old school when it came to Wine Club snacks and it always reminded me of coming home from college and Mom making me all my favorites even if it was just for a weekend. Today Peggy did not disappoint. Here is a sampling of her spread:

Bugles Stuffed with Pimento Cheese (Bugles haven't been on shelves in fifty years!)
Pigs in a Blanket
Swedish Meatballs
Homemade Chex Mix
Sour Cream and Chive Stuffed Celery Sticks
Turkish Delight (Pretty sure they're the same ones nobody's touched for over a year)

This had been billed as the "Abigail Rose Murder Investigation" Wine Club and everyone was in attendance. To my enormous relief, Penelope had handed me back the signet ring as soon as I walked in and told me she'd explain her findings when it was her turn.

Thankfully, Peggy's tastes for wine did not mirror her food choices or we'd be tippling Muscatel and Thunderbird. Instead Peggy had procured a tasty selection of First Class Pinot Noirs from Aconcagua, Chile. Light and easy-drinking, bottles were being opened faster than a kid's presents on Christmas morning.

"Okay, now that we've been amply supplied with fortification and energy it's time to review what we've got and what we need for the cops to make an arrest in Abigail's murder."

It appeared that Peggy was driving the bus today.

"Halsey, why don't you refresh our memories by reciting the suspect list," Peggy said.

"Okay, here's what we've concluded and why:

> *Malcolm:* Being Abigail's great grandson, he had the most to gain. I did some research and found that Abigail had two grandsons, Charles and Michael. Charles was Malcolm's father and as he told me, both his parents died in a car accident when he was young. Michael, his uncle, never married and there-fore had no heirs. And here's the kicker, he died last March, which was just before Malcolm appeared on Rose Avenue.

"Also, may I remind you that he is putting in a basement as part of the remodeling of the house he's inherited? Perhaps in anticipation of getting the deed to all the mineral rights?" Penelope said, proud of herself.

"So the motive's clear, but why not just wait Abigail out? She was not long for this world," Sally said.

"Good point." Peggy nodded. "Next suspect, Halsey."

> *Howard, the developer:* There are a lot of things that don't add up here. He too is putting in a

basement, as I know all too well. I can still taste that putrid muck. Someone started the rumor that he'd struck oil although he denies it. Why? Then there's the unfortunate demise of his workman, Carlos. Augie said that Howard had a clear alibi for the night Carlos was murdered, but that doesn't mean that he couldn't have hired someone else to do it. Until Augie gets the CSI and autopsy reports, Howard is very much still a suspect in Carlos's death.

"But how does he tie into Abigail Rose?" Penelope asked.

"Hasn't anyone noticed how little progress has been made on the site?" asked Paula. "Howard started construction three months ago and has very little to show for it. What if he really has found oil, and heard about the possibility of acquiring a deed for the whole pie? Malcolm may have been able to wait for Abigail's death, but Howard would need to steal it before anyone else got near it. Maybe he confronted her and tried to get the deed out of her hands and he went too far? Knocked her over or something?"

"Excellent deducing, Paula," I said. I was amazed at how lucid she was versus our last encounter in her gardens. I looked at Sally and could tell that she was thinking the same thing.

"Any others?" Peggy asked, passing bottles of wine around for refills. She already knew the answer to her question.

I took a sip of wine and continued.

Bobby Snyder, the ersatz lawyer: This one's like a rotten onion with layers and layers of lies to peel back. His name is actually Robert Snopes. He was a crooked ambulance chaser and he lied about his identity, probably to hide the fact that he's been disbarred from practicing law ever again. Augie says that he avoided jail time with bribes. It looks like this is his latest "get rich quick" grift, selling phony mineral rights packages he's "negotiated" and pocketing the money. He's somehow tied to Howard, for one thing we know that he was part of the argument they had with the workman, Carlos.

"But I'm guessing that until he actually makes a sale Augie has no cause to arrest him or even bring him in for interrogation?" Sally said.

That gave me an idea . . .

"For all we know Howard and this Snyder/Snopes could be in cahoots on the con," Peggy said. "Did you have another, Halsey?"

She knew I did, but I couldn't bring myself to list Max in front of Paula, especially now that I knew how fragile she was. Besides, the rest of us had already talked about this at lunch.

"Isn't that enough?" I sat down, now done with my presentation but continued speaking. "Paula, you mentioned that you would kindly share some of Max's research with us. Have you been able to procure any of his papers?"

"I do have them for you. If you follow me home

after Wine Club, I will give them over," Paula said, taking a gulp of her wine.

"So are we any closer to narrowing down the list of suspects?" Penelope asked.

"It sure doesn't look like it, this is more complicated than finding Waldo. Don't you think, Halsey?"

"It seems so, Sally, but I do have a plan."

"Perfect, lay it on us," Penelope said, and they all moved in close to me. Even Paula's face had lit up with excitement.

"Okay, first order of business is to get to the bottom of Howard's construction. We need to see the permits, find out how this project is being funded, and what sort of time frame they have committed to."

"I'm happy to go downtown and get copies of what the Los Angeles Department of Building and Safety has on file," Paula offered.

"Great. Peggy, can you follow the money trail?"

She nodded to me, and I saw her open up her contacts list on her iPhone.

"And, Penelope, Howard's never met you, correct?"

"Correct."

"Perhaps you could walk by the site, introduce yourself, and tell him you are interested in hiring him to remodel your house next. That way you can find out when he thinks that he'll be finished with the current one."

"And when you find out, add four months to that date." Peggy harrumphed.

"Any news on the deed and the ring?" Paula sat forward in her chair and looked directly at me.

"Excellent question, Paula," I said, wanting to include her and to reward her diligence. "The deed is with a noted historian friend who continues to perform his analysis." I decided to perpetuate this little white lie otherwise people would try to guess where I'd hidden it. I did make a mental note to follow up with Frederick Ott.

"What is his name? I wonder if Max knows him," Paula said.

"He preferred that I keep his name out of this at the moment," I replied, remembering that when you tell a lie the KISS principle is the order of the day: keep it simple, stupid.

"Of course." This seemed to fluster Paula, and she got up and went into the kitchen.

"What about the ring?" Sally asked.

I held it up and nodded to Penelope to present her findings.

"Firstly, the authentication process is almost but not entirely complete. According to my expert, Grace, the symbols on the band are Victorian although the metal is not pure gold. That doesn't totally disqualify the ring but it raises some suspicions."

Penelope took the ring from me and showed it to the group. The reverence with which she did this told me that she must be very good at her job as docent.

"If you remember Halsey telling us, there is an inscription on the inside. It says Memento Mori, 'Remember you will die.'"

"Such a lovely sentiment." My mouth had snuck ahead of my brain again.

"It's a matter of how you perceive the message; it could be taken to mean live your life to the fullest." Penelope smiled at me.

"Which you'd have to say Abigail Rose did, living well into her nineties," Peggy said.

"Until she was buried alive," practical Sally interjected.

"WHAT? I thought you said that someone murdered her and then buried her in the gardens?" Paula screamed.

I nodded to Sally, remembering that Paula hadn't been at lunch in the Marina when I told the other girls what Augie had said.

"I'm afraid so. Augie got back the autopsy report results, and it showed that she had died from asphyxiation; they found soil in her lungs. She had been alive when she was buried."

"No, no, NO!" Paula stood and paced in circles.

"Here we go again," Peggy said. Sally waved her to be quiet.

"Here, luv, how about a nice bit of Turkish delight?" Penelope soothed, offering a small plate.

Paula froze in place. She was visibly working on slowing her breathing and trying to calm herself. I stood next to her and put my hand on her shoulder.

"I—she was my next-door neighbor," Paula softly explained. "For so many years. I can't bear thinking that she suffered in any way. I miss her so."

"Peggy, it's time for that sickeningly sweet confection to hang up its cleats," Sally said, picking up the tray of Turkish delight. "It needs to ride off into the sunset on a camel, it would make anyone apoplectic."

"How about some more wine?" I asked Paula, filling her glass and sitting her back down.

She welcomed the gesture and took a much-needed mouthful.

"Penelope, was there more to report on the ring?" I'd decided to continue on with the meeting.

"A bit, yes. These engravings on each side, although a bit hard to define due to wear, are actually crude images of coffins."

This time when she passed around the ring everyone took a minute to study it.

"The etching on the lid of the locket part of the ring is a mirror image of a family crest, but Grace has not been able to trace its origin yet."

"Was there any trace evidence of poison from inside the locket?" I asked.

"That's really more something that the police labs should investigate, but Grace found none."

"Is that everything?" Peggy asked Penelope.

"Just one last bit, on the underside of the locket lid you can see a faint series of lines in the shape of a horseshoe. This was a common superstitious practice of the time, said to ward off demons and bring the wearer harmony, success, and happiness. This one had Grace scratching her head a bit."

"Why?" Sally asked, and we were all interested in her response.

"Well, it's just a bit of mixed metaphors. It seems like the jewelry designer was trying to cover all the bases and has added every kind of symbol."

"Interesting. Have you told Grace that the family name is Rose? Maybe that will help her trace the crest."

"I have, but no luck yet."

"Great job," Paula said, looking fully restored to her brand of normalcy.

"Sally, I've already commissioned Jack and his dog to pay Malcolm a visit," I said. "He plans to introduce himself and explain our connection and just say hello. The subtext being, 'don't mess with Halsey.' Perhaps you could play 'good cop' after Jack's visit, maybe bring him some of your yummy vodka drunken tomatoes and see what you can get out of him?"

"Can do, but I'll have to pick up more vodka."

And this is why I love Sally.

"What about the phony lawyer, Snyder?" Paula asked.

"Ah, he's been so persistent in trying to get my address so that he could drop by and tell me all about how rich I'm about to become that I thought I'd take him up on it. I might even be his first customer, record the whole transaction, and make it a sting operation."

"You can't do this when you are alone, Halsey. We already know the man can't be trusted," Peggy said.

"Well, I can't have any of you there, he'll know it is a trap. The same goes for Jack. I'll have Bardot with me, what could go wrong?"

"Everything," Sally said. "This guy will stop at nothing, he's shown that. He's so low you can see his feet in his driver's license photo."

"How about your neighbor, what's her name? Marisol. She could keep you company," Paula suggested.

I'd rather spin around thirty times and then run with scissors.

Chapter 16

"Hello, Mr. Snyder?" I asked although I recognized his nasal voice immediately.

"It is indeed, and to whom do I have the pleasure of speaking with?"

"My name is Halsey, I live on Rose Avenue. You might remember my dog Bardot? People forget me, but she leaves an indelible impression."

"Of course, of course. How could I forget a beautiful girl like yourself?"

I had to hold the phone away from my face for a moment. I knew I was imagining it but I could swear that I felt slime running down my hand and onto my arm. I had Max's research papers on the coffee table and put them out of sight in the middle of a thick Fall fashion magazine.

"How may I be of service, Miss Halsey?"

"I've read over the literature you gave me, and I'd like to learn more about procuring the mineral rights to my property. Would you be able to drop by at your convenience and walk me through the process?"

"Absolutely, let me check my calendar. Ah, it so happens that I had a rare cancellation for this afternoon, thus I could be at your lovely home within the hour."

Cancellation my butt, he's probably sitting right outside in his ratty car.

"That works for me." I gave him my address.

"Will your charming dog be joining us?"

"I can put her in another room," I replied, suspicious about why he was asking.

"Excellent, I shall see you shortly. How do you take your coffee?"

"I don't drink coffee, just bring yourself please."

Just after hanging up, I saw Marisol appear in the back at my patio doors. I grimaced remembering that she had keys to my house and could enter at will. Bardot greeted her like a long lost friend.

"You couldn't just ring the doorbell?"

"Course not, I didn't want anybody to see me. This is supposed to be a sting operation right?"

It was then that I noticed that Marisol was dressed in a nurse's uniform.

"What's with the costume, are you auditioning to be an extra on *General Hospital*?"

She pushed past me and into the house where she deposited a heavy-looking bag on my living room floor.

"Don't be ridiculous. I'm in disguise for the mission. If this creep tries anything, I'll be in like a flash."

"And do what? Listen to his lungs while he coughs?"

"And tell him that I'm your at-home nurse and he'd better leave because you are still contagious, that's what."

Not bad . . .

"Okay, but I doubt that it will come to that. Like we discussed, you are to stay in the bedroom with Bardot and make sure that we are recording all of this. Is that the equipment in that bag?"

She nodded and bent down to get started.

After Paula's kind but ill-conceived suggestion to involve Marisol, I got to thinking that I did in fact need her after all. But not for moral support, I needed her for her spying tools and capabilities.

I have to admit that it was quite hilarious to watch this senior citizen with her white tights and matching sensible shoes hide cameras around the living room and wire them to a receiver. She stopped after placing another camera and stared at a handful of wires. She seemed to be running through the sequence in her head. When she asked for a ladder, I put my foot down.

"Oh no, any climbing I'm doing. I don't need to have my 'nurse' lying on the floor with a dislocated hip while I'm trying to entrap Mr. Snyder, Esq. in the act of committing fraud."

"You'd fall before I would," Marisol said defiantly.

"And just how do you figure that?"

"You drink wine all day long. I'll bet you're seeing three of me right now."

"One more word and I'll be seeing zero of you.

He could be here any minute. You and Bardot need to disappear. Now! Is everything ready to go? It's all turned on?"

"Of course, this isn't my first rodeo," Marisol replied, taking one more look around. The receiver was hidden under a sofa and she could listen in through wireless headphones. "If I hear anything that sounds off, I'm calling Augie."

I wondered what she considered "off" but had no time to investigate. She and Bardot marched away to my bedroom.

"Don't go snooping in my stuff while you're in there."

"I wasn't going to but now that you mention it . . ."

I held back my yell just in time as the doorbell rang. From the set of three small windows in my wooden front door, I could see the straw bowler and the tips of some flowers.

Crap, he was going to lay it on thick.

Something in the back of my head made me pause. I had that nagging feeling that I was missing something. When the bell rang again, I gave up and went to the door.

"Mr. Snyder," I said. "Thanks for coming over."

"The pleasure is all mine. Since you don't drink coffee, I thought that these would offer some enjoyment although their beauty doesn't hold a candle to yours," he smarmed.

I think I threw up a little in my mouth. As I closed the door behind him, I caught sight of Peggy and Sally across the street pretending to be out for a fitness walk. The plan was that once Snyder left they would follow him either on foot or by car to see where he goes next. I saw Peggy's car parked out front. I felt a little better knowing that they were at the ready.

"We can sit in the living room," I said, guiding him to the seat where the cameras were pointed.

He removed his bowler and stood politely until I was seated. Once I did, he began his spiel.

"As you are aware, Miss Halsey, the house in which you reside is sitting atop enormous wealth with endless possibilities."

I gave him a blank, unimpressed stare. If he was planning to steal from me, he was going to have to work hard for it.

"Are you prepared to show me any sort of proof that there is oil in this land before I invest?"

"Right down to business, I admire that," he said. "I have brought some 'show and tell' for you."

He opened his weathered leather briefcase, and I could see that the lining had been shredded.

Even his cat must hate him.

"Proof number one." He produced a thick stack of long papers reminiscent of home sale closing documents. "This is the field inspection report conducted by our geophysicists. Their high-tech instruments take measurements and record data from deep under the property's surface. In the case of Rose Avenue, the vibration signals and empirical science tell us that there is a high probability that oil exists on your property. You can see that this study has been signed and certified."

Before I could pick up the document and read anything on it, Snyder returned it to his case. All I saw was a signature that wasn't legible and some kind of seal.

"I'd like to—"

"But this is only the tip of the iceberg," he interrupted me and pulled out a collection of stones wrapped in cloth. "These are called source rocks; I've got some limestone, black shale, and coal. All of these were taken from a nearby test site that we have constructed."

"And what, pray tell, do these indicate?" I asked, picking one of the larger ones up and feeling the heft of its weight. I was sick of watching this charade, but I needed to see it through in order to go to the cops. I put it down and went for the black shale, admiring its wafer thin layers and striations.

"I am so glad that you asked, Miss Halsey. You see, these rocks possess a high occurrence of hydrocarbon; in other words, oil and gas."

"How do you know this? Is there another document in there with a seal and a signature?" I asked, nodding with my chin to his briefcase.

"Nothing so pedestrian, Miss Halsey."

The magician reached back into his bag of tricks and this time presented some sort of version of a Geiger counter. It was yellow and looked like a toy from RadioShack.

"Why don't we just look at the contract, shall we?" My intelligence had been insulted enough.

But before I could stop him, he'd turned on the thing and was about to wave a wand over the rocks. It sounded like a combination of hail on concrete and a little child tap dancing. I was about to press again for the contract when he stopped over a couple of rocks that triggered the machine to wail like a herd of fire trucks. He must have discretely turned up the sound.

This wasn't going to end well.

The intrusive noise, as I knew it would, set Bardot off into a series of wolfish howls followed by overly loud shushing from Marisol.

"Is someone else here?" Snyder asked, returning his props quickly to his bag and rising from the chair. "Where's the dog?"

I guess Snyder realized that Bardot was not a fan. Jack had explained to me that sometimes when dogs hear sirens they think that the sound is coming from another dog. They answer back as a form of communication.

"You need to go out?" I heard Marisol say to Bardot, again not in a whisper.

"No!" I yelled and then heard Snyder do the same.

Too late, Bardot came bursting into the living room, bumping into Snyder who had made a fast dash to the door. He tripped and recovered, losing his hat in the process. Snyder exited the house with his briefcase, leaving his headwear as a casualty of war.

"I'll call you," I heard his muffled voice say from the other side of the door.

"What's with him?" Marisol said, trying on the bowler.

I looked at her in that silly thing and that's when it clicked.

Chapter 17

"We're having a sunset Wine Club in about an hour," Sally said to me over the phone the next day. "Want me to swing by and pick you up? Peggy and I have some good recon to report on Mr. Slimy Snyder."

"Great, and I do as well."

The "sunset" part of this Wine Club meant that we gathered at a specific location at a specific time. We usually did this in the summer when we wanted to change things up, and the general aviation, single runway Santa Monica airport played host. When Sally pulled up to my curb, I saw that she already had a full car. Paula was riding shotgun and Penelope and Peggy were in back. Sally drives a roomy SUV, so it was nothing for me to squeeze in with the girls.

My contribution today was ice-chilled Lillet. This is a French aperitif from Podensac, a small village south of Bordeaux. My introduction to this delicious potent potable came when I lived in NYC and in the summers used to frequent a very authentic Parisian bistro called La Goulue. It is light and aromatic, perfect for heat and humidity and is a blend of selected wines and macerated fruit liqueurs all crafted on site and then sent around the world. I like it just with ice, a wedge of orange, and a few fresh raspberries. But just about any fruit would bring out the best in this wine. Except kiwi, don't use kiwi. Trust me.

Our chosen watering hole to tie up to was the observation deck outside and above Typhoon Restaurant that sits directly on the side of the Santa Monica airport runway. It is open to the public, and the noise from the planes is mostly not a bother as the small aircrafts give off more putts and hums than rampaging roars. Besides having the privilege to witness the genius of the Wright Brothers over and over, at the western end of the runway is a gorgeous panoramic vista of the Pacific, and in the late afternoon, the setting sun. Hence the specific "place and time" caveat for this sort of Wine Club. There were tables and chairs on the deck, so we daisy chained what we needed and made ourselves at home.

Today the enticing sustenance was expertly prepared by Typhoon. The Pan-Asian appetizers included ahi tuna sliders, curried deviled eggs, Korean fried cauliflower, rice paper shrimp and vegetable rolls, and sweet potato fries with spicy ketchup. The Lillet was a perfect pairing as was the Japanese beer sampler flight courtesy of the restaurant.

We all settled in and let the beautiful environment warmly seep into our pores. As if on cue, a blue-and-white propeller-driven Cessna readied for takeoff at the east end of the airport. We watched as it gracefully accelerated on its three wheels, and when it was just about in front of us, the back end lifted first and then the nose. After a slight wobble, the plane righted itself and headed off into the beautiful, saturated blue sky.

"That never gets old," Peggy said. "I remember when I'd just started dating Vern, and he took me up in a little puddle jumper like that one. We ate dinner on Catalina Island and ended up staying the night."

"Peggy, you trollop," Penelope joked. "I bet it was fantastic."

"Which part?" Peggy riposted.

"First off, cheers," I interrupted. "To a fabulous end to a not so wonderful week, although things are looking up!"

The Lillet went down like caviar.

"I want to hear your report," I said to Peggy and Sally, "and then I'll add my news. I have a feeling that we are close to tightening the noose on our friends Howard the developer and Slimy Snyder."

"Well, we haven't definitively been able to tie the two crooks together, but what we've got seems awfully close to 'probable cause,' " Peggy said.

Sally pulled out her iPad and swiped until she found what she was looking for.

"While we were getting what we could online about Howard and his property, Paula went downtown and pulled copies of the records," Sally said, and Paula nodded. "Paula, why don't we begin with what you found out?"

Paula removed some official-looking legal-sized papers from what appeared to be a gardening tote because it was decorated on the outside with cartoony smiling flowers and had a series of long pockets for transporting planting tools. She laid the papers on the table and I quickly anchored them with the beer flight. Next she produced oversized folded plans and blueprints.

"Howard submitted these in May of last year and they were approved in September," Paula explained, pointing to some date stamps on the blueprint. "The start for breaking ground was to be January one of this year."

"Was there a completion date included?" I asked. We were all looking hard at the blueprint, but if the other girls were like me, they were still trying to figure out if the paper was upside down or right-side up. The confused looks on their faces told me I'd guessed correctly.

"There always is but it's a joke really, at least that's what the clerk told me," Paula continued.

"What was the date for this project?" I had moved to the other side of the table and was finally able to orient myself to what I was studying.

"That's the thing that struck the clerk as so odd, he said that completion dates range anywhere from eight months to two years. But in this case it was clearly stated that final inspection should be scheduled for the end of March."

"Just three months. I knew about developers making empty promises, but to build a house from the ground up in that short a period of time? That's crazy," Peggy said.

I pulled the blueprint closer to me and took a minute to really take it all in.

"Do you notice what's missing from this?" I asked.

They all pored over the paper, but again, I don't think that the drawing had become clear in their minds yet.

"The basement, where's the basement?" Penelope asked.

"Exactly," I said. "There is no indication here that they planned to dig any deeper than the foundation. We now know that all kinds of geological surveys and tests need to be done before getting a permit to dig."

"That could have delayed the start by months or even years," Paula said, turning the plan in her direction. I could tell that she was a little mad with herself for missing this detail.

"So the basement was going to be built under the radar, so to speak. But why?" Penelope squeezed an orange slice and the juice melded with her last two sips of Lillet.

"I think that we can give you some good reasons," Peggy said, and Sally woke up her iPad screen.

"It looks like Mr. Howard Platz was leveraged up to his beady eyeballs," Sally explained, showing us some sort of P&L statement.

"Where did you get this?" I asked.

Peggy waved me off and picked up the story. "Howard was running a construction Ponzi scheme. He was constantly borrowing from the next job to cover his overages and inaccurate estimates for the previous one. And the sums he owed have been growing exponentially."

"How much is he in the hole?" I asked.

"About one and a half million," Sally replied. "And naturally his suppliers and workers are the last to be paid, so he keeps having to find new ones."

"And if word got out on the street, then he'd be blacklisted and shut down." I saw everyone fall deep into thought.

We watched another small plane land. A couple and their son who looked about seven or eight disembarked once it had taxied to our side of the runway. They climbed the stairs and headed into Typhoon possibly for an early supper. It is amazing to me how inured I've become to witnessing these simple acts of shameless luxury.

"That's the reason he was building the basement without permits!" Paula was up on her feet and hopping with excitement. "He was and is hoping to strike oil. He needs that money desperately to get out of debt and has no time to lose. He probably knows about the deed. Maybe he's the one who murdered Abigail to get his hands on it."

"And while he was at it, he had to get rid of his workman Carlos. We were told that he would show up on the job drunk, and as you said, Halsey, Howard can't afford for any of his financial strife to get out." Penelope adeptly picked up four sweet potato fries in one hand, dipped them into equal amounts of ketchup, and gracefully popped them into her mouth. We know how much the Brits love their "chips." I was surprised that she hadn't gone on a search for malt vinegar.

"Do you think that we have enough to take to Augie?" Sally asked.

"How much of that can you share?" I asked, pointing to the spreadsheet on her tablet.

"We'll need a bit more time to pull together our sources." Peggy quickly stepped in and took the iPad from Sally.

I had thought as much. This info had all the earmarks of being accessed surreptitiously from one or more of her contacts in "The Company" aka the CIA.

"Okay," I said, "and while you are doing that, I think that I have a way to tie Mr. Slimy Snyder into the fold."

"I can't wait to hear." Paula was really enjoying all of our detective work, almost as much as she was enjoying the Lillet. When I saw her dipping a piece of Korean fried cauliflower into her glass, I discretely cut her off.

I recounted the visit that Snyder had paid me and watched them laugh when I described his pathetic attempt to authenticate his oil claims. They were still chuckling when I told them about "nurse Marisol" and her spying, and when I got to the Geiger counter and Bardot, they had escalated back to a full roar. At the end, Peggy and Paula had to excuse themselves to visit the ladies' room.

"So since he didn't get to make a sale with you, then we still don't have anything to prove he is running a scam?" Penelope summed up after they'd all calmed down and Peggy and Paula had returned.

"True, but remember I said that I thought that I had something to tie him to Howard? He'd run out of my house so fast to escape Bardot that he didn't even take the time to retrieve his derby hat. It was when Marisol tried it on for size that I remembered seeing something made of straw hanging on a nail at the construction site. It was under a jacket but I clearly saw it. This was the night that we discovered Carlos's body. I was so happy to get out of there that I just dismissed what I'd seen."

"So you think that it was Snyder's bowler hanging there?" Penelope asked.

"One of them. I looked up the brand of the one he left at my house and saw that you could buy these cheap things in packages of four on eBay."

"Glad you got something. Sally and I came up empty following him, the slime got into his car and drove off," Peggy said. "But I've made a note to check out Snyder's financial status very closely."

God help him.

"I'm going to make a quick trip back to the site after it is closed up for the day and see if the hat is still there. If it is, I'll take a few photos of it in place and then put it in a plastic bag to give to Augie."

"Not by yourself, I hope. That place is squirrelier than a nut factory." Sally was always watching out for me.

"I'll be in and out in a flash, I swear. Easy-peasy."

I later realized that saying this was akin to an idiot's last words which often are: "Hey, watch this!"

* * *

I took Bardot on a walk around the block at just about dusk and saw to my relief that Howard's site was locked up and quiet. We made the loop and then I let Bardot in through my back gate. On this occasion I was flying solo, this was a quick mission and no four-legged protection was going to be needed. I checked the blind slats in Marisol's windows and thankfully they didn't budge. Which didn't mean that she wasn't spying on me with cameras but this was the time that *Extra* aired, and Marisol had a little sumpin' sumpin' for Mario Lopez.

I wasn't expecting the gap in the fence that we got through last time to still be open. I was sure that Howard and his men had discovered it by now and stopped it up. I was prepared to do a little fence climbing, another reason why I had not brought Bardot. On my way I checked my pocket to make sure that I had the plastic bag I was going to use for the hat and the blue surgical gloves that I had swiped from my last doctor's visit.

You don't want me "borrowing" things? Then don't leave me alone in the examining room for forty minutes with last year's magazines.

Sure enough, the peeled back portion of fence to the back of the property was now closed off with builders' blocks that were too heavy for me to move. They were, however, great for climbing, and I used the hollowed-out sections as toeholds to help me easily climb to the top of the fence. Once there I stopped and listened to confirm that I was alone. Satisfied, I jumped down the six feet on the other side and was so focused on getting the evidence and leaving that I didn't stop to think about how I was going to get back out.

I used my phone for light and a quick look around showed me that no new construction had occurred since my last visit. Howard was probably putting all his efforts into finding oil, and I was anxious to see how much deeper the basement trench was now.

I entered the crude framed structure of the house, the sides still open to the air. To my left of the doorframe, I again saw the jacket hanging off a large nail. I opened my camera app, selected the flash option, and took several photographs. Each time the light went off, I could see the straw section of the hat brim underneath. When I was sure that I'd covered the scene in situ, I donned the gloves and lifted the jacket off the nail. I found another hook to hang it on and then examined the hat. I had photos of the one Snyder had dropped at my house and confirmed that they were similar. I repeated the same process of taking pictures of the evidence and when I was done, I took the hat and placed it in the plastic bag. I heard a car engine outside and froze. I tried to control my breathing while scanning for places that I could hide. After about three minutes all was still quiet and I let out a deep breath. If I was caught in here again, by anyone, I was toast.

I carefully placed the jacket back on the nail. I knew at this point that I should turn around and get out as fast as possible, but I was dying to take a look at the trench. Mostly I wondered if any more black sludge, possibly oil, had seeped into the hole.

If I could just get a sample of it, then we could

get it analyzed and know for sure if this was a scam. I put the bag with the hat down and ventured into the main section of the house frame. I treaded carefully using the light from my phone on the ground to make sure that I didn't accidentally fall in again.

When I got to the edge, I planted my feet firmly on the ground and scanned the trench. It was deeper, I'd say maybe four or five feet deeper. I had been thinking about how to get a sample of the sludge and had decided to use one of my surgical gloves as a scoop. The question was how to get down there and back up again. Toward the back, where I'd found Carlos's body I could see that a ladder had been placed along the muddy wall and was secured up top with sand bags.

Perfect.

I made my way to it, again stepping slowly to avoid slipping. Once there I tested the ladder and was relieved to see that it hardly budged from its place. It was now or never. With my back to the trench opening, I climbed down. The floor was even gooier and strongly clinging to my shoes and legs, making moving a labored effort. I decided to get my sample right where I was standing and get the hell out of there.

I needed to remove my glove carefully and inside out, I didn't want there to be any contamination from the outside elements that I had touched. This sounded easier than it was because my other hand was also gloved and I seem to have stolen—borrowed—a pair of extra larges. The surplus latex of the fingers kept getting in the way. I was finally successful and bent down to scoop up some of this potential black gold. When I was sure that I had enough, I removed the glove that was on my other hand and used my bare fingers to tie the open wrist portion of the glove with the oil sample.

Time to go home.

Before I could extract my feet and step on the bottom rung of the ladder, I heard voices coming from above. Then I saw the beams of flashlights moving in jerky arcs.

Crap.

I needed to think fast. I couldn't make out what the voices were saying, but I could discern that they were coming from men. Maybe some of the guys had forgotten their tools, or maybe they were gathering to get high, or for some other random reason. I figured that if I scrunched down on the floor in a far corner against the trench wall no one would notice me and I could just wait them out. I sunk into the viscous, sulfur-infused brew and cringed when I felt it seep through my pants. At least I hadn't done a face-plant this time. I tried to think of puppies and French Burgundy to pass the time. That's when the lights came on.

"What are you doing down there?" I heard a voice say but all I could see was the blinding yellow glow of a work light.

"Police," I heard another one say. "Don't move!"

As if I could . . .

Chapter 18

The short ride to the station did little to calm my nerves. First of all I was sporting new wrist bling courtesy of the LAPD that forced me to sit forward in the back seat of the cop car. I now have even less respect for anyone who has a handcuff fetish. Every time the car took a turn, I had no way of steadying myself and flopped over from side to side. Funny thing was it should be a straight shot from Rose Avenue to Pacific Division.

When we came to a stop, I looked out and saw a landscape of blue and white. This must be where the police cruisers go to sleep at night. There were sedans, vans, SUVs, and some motorcycles right around where we'd stopped, and in the darkness, my eyes easily tricked me into thinking that cops were hiding in them ready to fire if I made any wrong moves.

The guys that arrested me left me in the car and went inside through a metal back door. I swear they did this just to mess with me for presumably making their night shift longer. I was cold, wet, and ashamed. I never imagined that things could escalate so quickly. I kept hoping that Augie would open the car door and tell me this was all a misunderstanding and offer to drive me home.

That didn't happen.

When the officers returned, they helped me out of the car and walked me through the same metal door. On the other side was a hallway with concrete walls and floors and overhead fluorescent lights that would make even a beauty queen look like a crack addict.

They stopped me about six feet in and had me face a metal-gated window opening that led to another room. Everything that wasn't made of concrete was made of metal, some of it painted blue as if anyone needed reminding that they were in a police station. Another officer approached the window.

"We ask everyone who enters here the same three questions, Ms. Hall." This guy was large, and I could just tell that he gave out much more than he took in an altercation.

I stood flanked by the two arresting officers, who made sure that I was paying close attention. This was all too real. Here I stood handcuffed, my arms held by cops, in a hallway with nowhere to run. That's when I noticed the bench. It looked like it could seat four or five, it was metal of course and mounted to the floor in the center of the hallway. The front of the bench included a pipe that ran the length of it and had one part of a set of handcuffs attached to it. The bright, shiny stain-

less steel of the whole contraption made me think
I was about to get a Pap smear in a house of hor-
rors.

"Question one," the officer behind the cage
began. I looked at his shirt tags and saw that he
was something called a "Watch Commander."

"Do you understand why you are here?"

A voice in my head was telling me that these are
rhetorical or "yes" or "no" questions, so I con-
trolled my tongue and just nodded.

"Question two, are you sick, ill, or injured in any
way?"

"I will carry the emotional scarring of my way-
ward roguery to my grave, Watch Commander."

I felt one of the cops jab me in the back and
shut my mouth.

Not knowing what to make of my statement he
continued.

"Question three, do you have any questions?"

"Just the obvious one, sir. What happens next
and how do I atone?"

It was the middle of the night, and I could tell
from the way he looked at me that I'd better
change my tone before I had any chance of aton-
ing.

"I just mean, I have never experienced anything
like this, and I feel so sorry for both taking up your
valuable time and for trespassing on that almost
empty lot."

"We will now review the evidence and I will hear
the officers' reports and then we will decide how
to proceed, Ms. Hall. I understand that there is
some evidence to be booked and secured with the

property department?" he said, looking at one of the cops.

"Yes," the officer replied and held up an evidence bag. Inside was one of the blue surgical gloves I had used to take a sample of Howard's sludge. In this light, it looked like one of those blue doggie doo-doo clean-up bags filled with, well, doo-doo.

The watch commander made a face that told me he thought the same thing. "You can put her in Tank 2 while we review the case."

My stomach sank, I wasn't sure what "Tank 2" meant, but I was pretty sure that I wasn't about to get an MRI. We walked past the steel bench, thankfully, and then a room with a window and the prerequisite metal door. On it was a sign that said TANK 1. Staring back at me was a guy, more like a kid really, with blank eyes. Whether unconsciously or as a defense mechanism, he had made himself numb to his surroundings. All I could think was that he was too young to have had to learn to do that.

"In here," said the officer, less than gently guiding me into Tank 2. True to its secondary nature this one was smaller and the window was no larger than the pillow I wished that my head was laying atop. The same kind of fluorescent light lit the cell and another steel bench ran the length of the back wall. At least I was alone. I hoped.

Everything changed when the door closed.

The first thing that I noticed was the absence of sound. In any other situation, I would have welcomed the silence after all the police radios and commotion, but now it was a reminder that I was no longer part of things, interacting with the human race. The second thing I noticed was the inside surface of the door to the tank. Where there should have been a handle, there was instead a metal plate covering the hole from the inside. Predecessors had made attempts to scratch words, drawings, and symbols into the paint of the door. Crude scratches made me think of an insane asylum.

I had remembered a story I'd been told when I lived in New York City of a reporter who had decided to go undercover and live the life of a homeless person for forty-eight hours. It had been billed as an incredibly raw and brave piece of journalism particularly because the reporter was a woman. I thought so as well until I heard that a camera crew was with her filming the entire time. So she did have a lifeline. When I watched it, I was struck by something she said late at night when she was huddled in a doorway: "I am cold, I am uncomfortable, but I still can't image what it must feel like to be homeless because I know I have a key in my pocket and I know that in a short time I'll be able to go home."

Tonight I had no such assurances, and I had no idea if or when I'd be able to go home. I sat on the hard bench and leaned against the V-shape that the side and back walls made. My hands were still cuffed.

About an hour later I heard a key turn in the lock to my door and then it opened. The same arresting officer escorted me out of the cell and walked me back to the caged window where the watch commander was waiting. I let out a breath when I saw that his resting face this time did not appear to resemble someone's who'd eaten one of those long, thin red peppers that they put in Chinese food that you are supposed to discard.

"You're an interesting one, Ms. Hall. I see from various notes in our system that this is not the first time that you have pushed your boundaries and fallen under suspicion for a crime."

Don't talk, Halsey, I mean it!

"Here's where we've come out on this," he continued. "The California criminal justice system classifies crimes into three categories: the most series are felonies punishable with prison sentences."

I visibly shivered.

"This is not the case with you," he quickly told me.

Was I starting to gain his sympathy?

"The next down are misdemeanors, these crimes are punishable by a maximum of one year in county jail."

My mind immediately went to losing my dog, my house, and Jack. I could taste bile in my mouth and I must have gone very pale.

"Why don't you sit down on the bench, I know it's been a long night."

I did what he asked and stared at the extra handcuff attached to the bar. I started to shed small tears that stung my eyes as they fell.

"I think we can uncuff her, Officers. In your case, Ms. Hall, you have committed what is called an 'infraction,' the most common of these are moving violations like speeding or making unsafe turns. Non-criminal trespassing also falls into this category. Since it appears that you were not at this building site to cause any damage or to threaten anyone, you are not subject to incarceration or to being placed on probation."

"Thank you." I let out a deep sigh of relief.

"You do however have to pay a fine; in this case, the amount is one hundred fifty dollars. Do you have someone who can come and make this payment?"

I nodded.

"Good, as soon as they do, we can release you. Is there someone that you would like us to call?"

I gave him Jack's cell phone number. The back door opened and I saw officers bring in three very rowdy men. They reeked of alcohol.

"Best place for you to be until he arrives is back in the tank," he said as one of the guys spat at the caged window.

I didn't argue.

"Someone here to pick you up, Ms. Hall. You'd better be nice to him 'cuz he paid your fine," a different officer told me while unlocking the cell door. "Come with me."

The mud and sludge from the basement pit had now dried on my pants and when I stood, it made a cracking sound. It also made walking a conspicuous event as with each step a clump of it would fall off me and turn to a splat of dust when it hit the ground. I looked like Pig-Pen's deranged sister. And to top it off, I was shaking uncontrollably from a deep bone chill. It was five a.m.

The three guys that had been brought in were now cuffed to the center hall bench. I guessed that this was not their first time, as it hadn't shaken their attitudes or foul mouths. When we rounded the corner out to the sergeant's front desk, I saw Jack. I couldn't help it; I burst into tears. I'm talking major waterworks. So much so that I could feel the mud melting off in the narrow paths that the tears were marking. I imagined that my face must make me look like *Pagliacci*'s clown.

I reached out to hug him and the officer held me back. I could also swear that I saw Jack recoil a bit.

"Ms. Hall, I'm going to explain a few things to you," the sergeant said to me from his high desk pulpit.

"Yes, your honor," I whispered.

"Sergeant, it's just sergeant. Now, you were brought in on a suspected charge of criminal trespassing on private property. We have since downgraded this to an infraction. With the payment of this fine, you are exonerated. Do you know what that means?"

I nodded.

"You were lucky that the CSI officers that found you sorted this whole mess out."

"CSI? I thought that someone had reported seeing me on the property."

"Incorrect, the investigators were called back to the scene to gather further evidence as a result of the autopsy report on the dead workman."

"The results are back? May I see? What did the report say?"

"Halsey!" Jack admonished. I'd never seen him look at me that way. He was seething mad.

"This is exactly the kind of thinking that got you here in the first place. This is not your business and you need to stay out of it. Understood?" the sergeant asked.

I was about to say that it was very definitely my business if I was a suspect in the murder, but stopped myself. If Augie had really made that official, then this would be a moot point anyway. Instead, I nodded vigorously to the man on high.

"Mr. Thornton was kind enough to pay the small amount with the promise that you will leave here never to return again. You will mind your own business, be a law-abiding citizen of Mar Vista, and an example for all to follow. Which you vow to do, correct?"

"Yes I do, your honor, I mean sergeant. May I get my personal belongings back? I believe that they were placed in the property room."

He eyed me for a while and then picked up the phone. A couple minutes later a female officer came out with the evidence bag containing my blue gloves of sludge.

"Thank you, thank you so much!" I said finally feeling the light at the end of the tunnel.

"Thank Mr. Thornton, without him you'd have been locked up until morning."

I reached to put my arms around Jack.

"Are we cleared to go, Sergeant?" Jack asked.

"Go, and get some sleep."

Jack took my arm and we exited the station.

"Honey, I am going to make you the best breakfast ever for getting me out of that nightmare. I think that bacon and sausage is in order. We could also start with prosciutto and melon. Do you want French toast or pancakes? I hope I have some champagne chilling."

"This is all fun and games to you, Halsey, isn't it? You think that this is a lark, being arrested in the middle of the night? Maybe the cops have nothing better to do?" He was not happy.

"Well, I thought I brought some levity to the station. How about I bring them a basket of bagels in the morning, donuts would be so, obvious."

When we approached his monster truck, he opened the back door first, leaving me wondering if he was going to drive me home in a doggie crate. To my relief, he had retrieved a couple of big towels.

"Wrap yourself in these," he said, tossing them to me. "You're a dirty mess and I don't want it to get all over my vehicle."

"Jack, I'm sorry," I said, doing as he'd commanded. He unlocked the doors, and I was careful to take off my shoes and slap them against each other to shake off the mud before I got in the passenger side. "I was just trying to get a sample so it could be tested for oil. I didn't mean any harm."

"You never do, Halsey. But it's always one more little thing and the next we know you're in jail or kidnapped or stowed away on a boat."

"That was part of the kidnapping."

"Whatever, I don't find this fun or funny. I have

a relatively calm life training dogs and the excitement comes when I'm called on a rescue with CARA. And then I am working for a good cause to rescue someone and prevent further danger. I am not running after some pie-in-the-sky theory about striking oil and moving to Beverly Hills."

"When did I ever say that? And I resent you calling what I am doing just a lark. You need to remember that I'm a suspect here, for two murders! Do you think that I planned to find Abigail's body in the garden? Do you, Jack?"

We rode the rest of the way in silence until we pulled into my driveway.

"I don't know anymore. These things always seem to happen to you," he said, not looking at me.

"Wait here a minute, please," I said and got out of the truck. A couple of minutes later I returned. He'd rolled down the window on his side, and I handed him two hundred dollars.

"I think that this covers the fine and the gas it took for you to come and pick me up. There should also be enough left over for a nice breakfast. Thanks, Jack."

"Let's just take a breather for a little bit, okay?" He put the truck in reverse and was slowing backing out. "I love you, Halsey, very, very much."

"You love sedate, wine-infused Halsey. Too bad because today kick-butt Halsey came out to play."

I watched him drive away and went into the house where Bardot was beside herself with kisses for me. The sun was just coming up. I opened the doors to the backyard. "Come on, Bardot!"

I took off running and jumped in the pool, clothes, shoes, and all. Bardot was right behind me.

"Where were you all night?" I heard a voice say from over the fence.

"In jail," I replied.

"Fine, don't tell me."

"I just did, Marisol."

Chapter 19

This time tequila shots were not involved.

I met Frederick Ott for coffee, tea in my case, the next day at the Rose Café, in Venice. This spot has been a favorite of the bohemian artists and the beach community since 1979. The café was recently renovated and under new ownership. It boasts a top chef causing walk-ins to be an exercise in futility. But we were there at an odd hour and were lucky to find a café table for two.

"People are going to think that I'm filthy rich." Frederick smiled, adding a sugar packet to his cappuccino.

"I thought you are," I teased.

"Hardly." He laughed. "But when they take note of my beautiful table companion it will be the only logical explanation."

I forced a smile. I'd taken two showers and a long bath after getting home from the police station, but I still felt like the unwashed.

"You don't seem your chipper self," he said,

noticing my somber demeanor. "Should we go find a place that serves midmorning tequila shots?"

"God no, I may never drink again."

"That would be a shame. So, Halsey, what has got you in such a funk as the beach people call it?"

Although encroaching on eighty years old, Frederick took pride in making an effort to stay current. That was one of the things I loved about him.

I gave him a recap of my trespassing arrest and my night in the holding tank while at the same time bringing him up to date on the Abigail Rose murder case. I told him that the sudden interest in oil rights in Mar Vista might be somehow connected to the deed I'd found with poor Abigail's body.

"Sounds like you have indeed poked the bear," he said when I'd finished. "I know I'll sleep better knowing that you have strongman Jack by your side."

I felt the blood drain from my face.

"Uh-oh, trouble in paradise? Dear, dear."

"It's all my fault," I started to explain.

"That, Halsey, is never the case. It takes two to tangle as I like to call it."

I brought Frederick up to speed on the fight and Jack's desire to "take a break for a while."

"I think that may be a good idea," Frederick finally said after a good several minutes of thinking. "You need to recognize that in much of Jack's world he has adopted the pack mentality. This is what he taught us while taming our savage beasts. He said that we needed to be the alpha dogs in our little pack at home in order for our dogs to respect us so that we could train them and manage their well-being. And do you know what? It worked. I was amazed, especially since one of our dogs outweighs my wife."

"I am very happy for you, dogs are such great partners. But I'm not sure where you are going with this in Jack's and my situation." I sighed.

"Forgive the pun, Halsey, but you are a strange new animal to Jack. He can try to be the alpha dog, but you do not possess the inner workings to be submissive and a follower. You wouldn't be happy in that position and neither would anyone else that knows and loves you. Especially Jack."

"Sooo?"

"So Jack needs time to adjust to this new kind of relationship. He's not the type to need to be controlling but it is the part of him that he goes to for peace and order in his life. I take it he's told you about his father?"

"Yes. I know that he'd been a forest ranger who worked search and rescue in Colorado. I also know that his dad died in the process of saving a family and their two young boys from a rafting accident. Jack was ten; the day he died was his birthday."

I closed my eyes for a moment to remember when he had told me this. We were on the beach in Malibu with the dogs when our relationship had just started. I could feel the tears trying to escape from my closed lids, and I could still feel the hurt I'd felt for his pain.

"Knowing those deep feelings Jack carries around should help you to help him adjust. He loves you very much, Halsey, that I know." Frederick sipped the remains of his coffee, giving him a foam mustache. "Maybe you need to just throw him a bone from time to time," he said with a mocha grin.

"Okay, that was one pun too many." I laughed. "But thank you for your valuable advice, Frederick. Switching gears, do you have any more information on the deed that I found?"

"I do, although it may not be what you want to hear. It is looking more and more like it is a very clever fake. For one, our research hasn't been able to turn up any provenance whatsoever. While the names of the signatories are those of real people who were alive at the time that the document was drawn, we cannot find any kind of trail to support its validity."

"Interesting, I've been given similar results by experts who have been analyzing the ring."

"Don't get me wrong, if this is a forgery, it is an excellent one done by someone with experience at these things."

For whatever reason, my mind went to Malcolm.

"I won't say that we've exhausted all possibilities, but we are getting close, Halsey."

"I completely understand and I can't thank you enough for all your hard work. You're the one who is a treasure, Frederick."

"You are too kind, my love." He beamed.

I reached in my bag for my tinted lip balm. I just loved that "kiss of cherry."

"Do you have anyone I could contact that tests soil samples for oil?" I pulled out the evidence bag and placed it on the table.

People who noticed the blue plastic with the brown sludge inside clearly thought that this was something entirely different and gave me a less than favorable reaction.

"I will see to it." He quickly put the baggie into his tweed jacket pocket.

That only exacerbated the looks of horror.

"He's going to test it for me," I explained to a couple that was openly staring at us. "I'm hoping it's positive!" I smiled.

When I got home, I called Peggy and Sally and asked them to come over. It had felt good to tell Frederick about my ordeal, but if I really wanted to vent, I needed my girls.

"And that's how you left it?" Sally asked when I'd finished my story.

"I'm afraid so. Frederick thinks that he just needs time, but I don't know."

"I agree with Frederick," Peggy said. "You're a dynamo, Halsey, and I'll bet that Jack's not the first one who's tried unsuccessfully to tame you."

I thought of my ex-husband and nodded.

"Maybe this will help you get your mind off Jack." Sally pulled out her trusty iPad.

"You bet it will. We've uncovered some very interesting new financial information about Howard the developer." Peggy paused for the tablet to boot. "And, your discovery of the straw bowler at his site confirms that Slimy Snyder is working right along beside him."

"Howard Platz had a development company with a different name that he ran into the ground, forcing him to declare bankruptcy a few years back." Sally showed me a PDF of a legal document. "His current company, the one named on the signs posted around his site is actually registered to a conglomerate out of Las Vegas."

"It is an actual LLC, I had someone check for me," Peggy added, "but it is very likely that most of the members of this group are bogus. What Howard is trying to do is skirt around the slow task of re-establishing credit that is needed to borrow money. Even when he does, the interest rates will be much higher until he can prove himself."

"Does anyone else feel like wine should be involved in this conversation?" I asked.

"Good lordy, yes, what took you so long?" Sally followed me into the kitchen to get the glasses.

When we returned, Peggy was thumbing through one of my magazines. She pulled out some papers wedged between the pages.

"What's this you're hiding, Halsey?"

"I forgot all about that, it's Max's research as provided by Paula. I hid it just before Snyder came in with his sales spiel."

"Perfect, we'll have to compare this with what Aimee found over the internet, but let's finish with Howard first," Peggy said, nodding to Sally.

I poured a Joel Gott Alakai Grenache; I loved its ripe fruit flavors reminiscent of France's Rhone Valley offerings. I'd discovered it when I was invited to a dinner party featuring Indian food. I'd thought that the light blueberry and raspberry notes complemented the spiciness of the food.

"It is like we said earlier, Howard is running a Ponzi scheme to keep afloat, but it is not helping. Enter Slimy Snyder. Either together or apart, these two created this mineral rights scam to raise money to save them and the project." Sally took a healthy gulp of her wine.

"So the basement that was not in the plans could have been an afterthought to make this scam credible," I said, thinking out loud. "If they'd really thought there was oil under there, wouldn't they have quietly dug until they found it?"

"Possibly, but if they were really out of money, then there isn't much they could do." Peggy frowned.

"Until they find the deed. Once they have that, they could borrow anything they want against it," Sally said. "But where does this take us? They could be guilty of a scam, but we have nothing to connect them to Abigail."

I agreed. *More tail chasing.*

"But Malcolm as they say had means, motive, and opportunity." A hundred thoughts started racing through my head. "What do we know about his ancestors? He said that they were some of the first settlers in America from England but after that, the story doesn't pick up until almost present day."

"What are you thinking, Halsey?" Peggy replenished my wineglass.

"Just wondering really. Penelope's expert for the ring and Frederick for the deed are close to confirming that both items are excellent forgeries. Since they were found together, I think it's safe to assume that they were done by the same person or persons."

They nodded.

"To forge both, a person would have to have deep historical knowledge as well as the skills in printing with the tools of the 1900s. They would also have to be a jewelry expert and designer. In other words, if someone would go to this much effort to create these, then it seems likely that he or she would also kill for the mineral rights if it came to that."

"Are you liking Malcolm for this, Halsey?"

"No, Peggy, I think that we have to go further back. I remember the older Coast Guard captain telling me that after Abbot Kinney built his renaissance dream in Venice that the carnival people came in to take advantage of the crowds he'd drawn."

"So, con artists," Sally said. "Time to see if young Malcolm has some swindlers in his past."

She was already starting a search on her tablet.

"I'm impressed; we are getting closer. The last thing for today I think is to look through the document Paula gave you," Peggy said doing just that.

"I'm doing this from memory, but I've been told that I have a mind like a steel trap."

"Remind me never to get totally drunk with you, Peggy."

"Ah, interesting," she said after a couple of minutes.

Sally and I both looked at her.

"The whole section about the woman murdered up in the gardens is missing. That took up about three pages in the digital file, right?"

"Right," I said.

"Well, these pages are numbered and after page sixteen it skips to page twenty."

"So Max must have removed them not knowing that the report was already online," Sally said.

"Or maybe Paula," I said.

I cannot possibly tell you why but I found myself knocking on Marisol's door. Her brand of wackiness was just what I needed to keep my mind off my woes. I know I'm in trouble when the wine stops working.

"What?" I heard from behind the dark metal screen door.

"I brought some of that cheese you liked at my house and some crackers."

"Okay, you can come in, but don't dillydally, just tell me what you want."

She stood aside and I walked through and into her living room. I looked at the framed family photos displayed on every surface and remembered the night she'd told me about her husband.

"I don't got any wine, if that's what you're looking for," she said.

I smiled. "No, I don't want any wine."

"You got a fever? Should I call 9-1-1?"

"No, I'm fine. May I?" I asked, motioning to the powder-blue sofa. She nodded.

"I'll get some plates and paper napkins."

While she was gone, I looked again at the wedding photo sitting over the mantelpiece and remembered the conversation:

* * *

"My family came to America in 1940. I was ten," Marisol began. *"Javier's family, the same thing. We'd grown up on the same street in Mexico.*

"We did two big things when we turned eighteen. We became American citizens and we got married.

"In 1951 Javier was sent to Korea. He was so proud to be fighting for America; he wore that damn uniform even before he needed to.

"He got shot one week before he was coming home.

"He had a bullet in his spine and them doctors said it was too dangerous to operate. He came home in a god-damn wheelchair.

"He couldn't work; he couldn't play with his girls, we couldn't—

"One day he said he was going to lunch with a friend who came by and picked him up. Another guy back from Korea. I'd never seen him or heard about him before.

"He never came back."

"You sure I don't need to call a doctor or something? You don't look so good," she said, returning with plates, napkins, and two bottled waters.

"I'm okay. I suppose you know that Jack and I had a fight?"

"Oh no!"

"Marisol?"

"Okay, so I may have heard something about it. Was this on account of you getting arrested for trespassing?"

My head snapped in her direction. I'd told her I'd spent the night in jail but that was it.

"Augie told me, he's worried about you."

"Isn't there some kind of arrestee/police confidentiality that he has to follow?"

"Guess not. Don't worry about Jack, he's just worried about you."

"Have you talked to him?"

The train was definitely off the tracks.

"I remember when my second cousin Manny, they live in Pacoima, came over to spend the weekend. His parents needed to make a quick trip to Mexico and back for a death in the family," Marisol went on.

"You haven't answered my question!"

"We were just kids and I was very into climbing trees."

"All the better to spy on people, you started young. Can we get back to Jack?" My patience was fading fast.

"Hello, Auntie," Augie said, letting himself in. "Ah, Halsey, just the person I needed to talk to," he added, noticing me.

"Why not just tell Marisol like always? It'll get back to me soon enough."

"Look, I'm sorry that I wasn't there when you were brought in, Halsey, although there wouldn't have been much I could have done to help. You got off with a fine, you should be very thankful for that."

"Her boyfriend left her," Marisol said. Augie appeared caught off guard.

I gave her a serpentine eyes look.

Was she trying to set me up with Augie?

"You said that you needed to talk to me about

something, Augie?" I wanted to get the heck out of here.

"Yes," he said, sitting down and helping himself to the cheese plate. "Very good, Auntie."

Marisol beamed and I gave her the snake eyes again.

After another helping, he finally started talking.

"We've gotten the autopsy report back on Carlos, the workman found dead on Howard's construction site."

"I'd heard that but nobody would tell me the results."

"He died of an overdose of Methamphetamine mixed with alcohol."

"So he wasn't murdered?" I asked.

"Sounds like he murdered himself," Marisol said, disgusted.

"Correct, that was not a homicide, but he sustained a deep head wound prior to his death that is consistent with an assault with a large, sharp rock."

"How can they distinguish an assault from him hitting his head? You remember he was lying face-down in the basement pit?" I was very careful not to say, "When I found his dead body," which I had.

"The circumference of the wound itself shows blunt force different from what it would look like if he'd fallen onto a rock."

"So what does all that mean?" I asked, and Marisol nodded. She needed answers.

"That's what the officers were doing when they caught you back on the property the other night. They'd been sent to secure the crime area in advance of the crime scene investigators who were coming back to collect some rocks the size and description from the autopsy report to bring back for testing."

"So, what does this have to do with me besides being in the wrong place at the wrong time?" I was beginning to get that feeling in the pit of my stomach.

"That's the unfortunate news I have for you. Your fingerprints were found on a large piece of limestone that the CSU recovered, remember that we have them on file from the last time."

"Again, so? You know that I'd been down there, how else would I have found the body?"

"Understood, and the first time we investigated the scene, we concentrated on collecting evidence of a perpetrator. It was only after the autopsy report that we were tipped off to look for a rock like this one."

Augie showed us a photo of the rock on his phone. "It was the only one we found with your fingerprints on it. If you were crawling around in the dark, it is highly unlikely that you would have touched just one rock that night, Halsey."

Augie showed us a photo of the rock on his phone.

Marisol got up from her chair and turned on her TV. Was my fate that boring to her? She needed to see if *Family Feud* was on?

Augie seemed oblivious to her and continued, "Look, Halsey, I know that you wouldn't hurt anyone, at least I think so. And I know that you've been through the wringer, which is why I convinced the commander to let me come here and bring you in myself. We'll make you comfortable and have this cleared up in no time."

"No! I cannot go back there; I'm already scarred for life. This time I demand a lawyer."

Augie was about to speak when we heard a loud siren being emitted from the speakers hooked up to Marisol's TV. We both stared at her, and she turned it down and proceeded to rewind the picture. I looked at the screen and recognized bits of my living room going by.

"Let me see that picture of the stone again, Augie." Marisol grabbed the phone from him. "Now watch this."

She hit "play" and the video showed Slimy Snyder sitting on my sofa, his array of phony evidence had been laid out across my coffee table.

"But this is only the tip of the iceberg," you could hear him say as he presented his collection of stones wrapped in cloth. "These are called source rocks; I've got some limestone, black shale, and coal. All of these were taken from a nearby test site that we have constructed."

We watched as Snyder unwrapped the rocks and placed them in front of me.

"And what, pray tell, do these indicate?"

You could clearly see me picking one of the larger ones up and feeling the heft of its weight.

Marisol froze the video frame and held up the photo from Augie's phone beside it.

Augie and I gaped.

"Now, Augie, be a good boy and go back to your people and tell them that they'd better hurry and arrest this Snyder before he uses his slime to get away. Go, I'll email this video to you."

"Yes, Auntie Marisol," he said and dashed out.

"Marisol, do you really think that Snyder staged this entire show and tell at my house just so that he could get my prints on that rock? And then go back and plant it at the site? He stood to gain more by selling me a mineral rights package. Unless of course, he somehow murdered Carlos, supplied the drugs or something."

"That guy's slimy but he's also dumb as bait. Plus, he's too much of a wimp for murder. I think he needed to grab some rocks for his scam, took them from the site, and then tossed them back at the end of the day. Skinny runt like him could hurt his back carrying around that weight. Besides Augie has the video now."

"I shudder to think what I'm going to owe you for this." I gave Marisol a hug.

"You are right to be afraid." She gave me a gold-toothed grin.

Chapter 20

Walking along Rose Avenue always gave me a sense of calm and belonging. Every house looked welcoming and gave a hint as to what was happening with the people inside. The Millers were having their windows replaced, two doors down, the grass was being taken up to make way for a drought tolerant rock and succulent garden. I noticed that the training wheels were finally off one of the kid's bikes.

All this should have put me in a better mood but I'd had three hours of sleep last night and was operating on fumes. I should have slept like a baby knowing that Augie and his team had Snyder in custody and were hopefully roping Howard into the case they were building.

But despite my warm, furry bedmate, I couldn't stop thinking about Jack. Now more than ever I needed to feel centered and focused on the things that really matter. All qualities that came naturally to him. Instead, I had this nagging feeling that everything was about to implode. I've had this before and have even given it a name: "impending doom."

I tried to shake it off and put on a happy face as I entered Penelope's house.

"Augie, let me put you on speaker, I'm with the girls and they all want to hear the latest," I said, doing so and placing my phone on Penelope's coffee table.

Penelope was hosting Wine Club that afternoon and it was her first time, so she'd gone all out. Lest you think that meant little cucumber sandwiches with the crusts cut off and scones because she's English, you'd better think again. Penelope had been a world traveler as a student and was drawn to exotic locations and cuisines. Case in point, today we were treated to Vietnamese finger foods.

Penelope had a tray of rice paper spring rolls filled with veggies and mint served with a tangerine dipping sauce. There were fried wontons with a sweet and sour hot mustard sauce, pickled scallions and spicy prawns, and some sort of rice teacake that melted in your mouth. Her house was equally decorated with souvenirs she'd picked up while globetrotting. I saw old-looking batik fabric that was placed behind glass in a simple frame. There were several lengths of kukui nut leis from Hawaii hanging on a peg and a tapestry with religious art that looked like it could be from the Cru-

sades. There were many other fascinating items
that I couldn't identify, and I made a mental note
to ask her about them later.

"Augie, say hi to Sally, Peggy, Paula, and Penelope. You said that you had an update on this
Slimy Snyder character?" I said.

"Yes, I do. First of all we dusted the rock for
other fingerprints in addition to yours and we got
a match with Snyder's. He'd been in the system
from an old arrest back in his ambulance chasing
days. That gave us enough to bring him in for
questioning. He admitted that he and the developer, Howard, worked together on a real estate
project but denied that any part of the mineral
rights acquisition business was a scam. Since he
never got to complete a transaction with you or
anyone else for that matter, there is nothing to
prosecute. He still maintains that you are all sitting
above vast amounts of oil."

"I may have been born at night, but it wasn't last
night," Sally said. "That guy needs to learn a new
song."

"What did he say about his fingerprints being
found on the rock? Was he there that night with
Carlos?" Peggy asked.

"He denies being anywhere near Carlos that
night or any other. As for his prints, he says that he
had taken samples from the basement trench for
his sales presentation but that one was too heavy to
keep lugging around, so he tossed it back." Augie
sounded tired.

*Just as Marisol had called it. How far did her spying
really extend?*

"That's about all we've got, Halsey, I'm afraid that this is a dead end. We know it was drugs and alcohol that killed Carlos, and frankly, I believe that Snyder and Howard had nothing to do with it. They may be scammers but that's as deep as they go. For now, naturally we'll still keep an eye on them."

I had to agree but I hated it.

"If I remember correctly, Howard was caught with marijuana on him when he was a teenager working as an apprentice," Paula said.

That perked us all back up again.

"You should check the records, Augie; this would have been around 1975." Paula was suddenly a font of information.

"Good to know, but doubtful that I'll find anything. He'd have been arrested as a juvenile and those records often get expunged. If you're implying that Howard may have supplied this Carlos with the drugs, that's a stretch, but I'll follow up. Have a nice afternoon, ladies."

With that the call disconnected.

"Wow, Paula, great save," Peggy said.

"Yes, how on earth did you dig that out of the old attic?" Sally asked.

Emboldened, Paula poured herself another glass of wine.

Today Penelope was featuring a Francis Ford Coppola Sofia Rosé. Yes, that Coppola. It was the perfect accompaniment with its excellent concentration of fresh, juicy fruit flavors.

"I just remembered you telling me that Howard had worked for the neighborhood's old contractor, Sam, when he was just starting out in the business. Sam had built our pergola over the back patio and I'd remembered him saying how disappointed he was in Howard. He told us the whole story. He said the kid was already a real hustler."

Geez, these people are harder to nail than Jell-O to a wall. I resolved to amp up my efforts in this investigation. I was tired of the merry-go-round. It was time to hit the roller coaster.

The next day, I decided to pay Paula's husband, Max, a visit at the small office they rent for the local historical society. This was my chance to talk to him without Paula being present. Plus, I'd been told that it was a really cool place.

The "office" was actually one big room that sat above the carport of one of the oldest homes on Grandview Blvd. The street was so named because it provided views of both the ocean to the west and the mountains to the east. It ran parallel along the top of the gardens and baseball fields. The only way to tell that the place existed was by reading a small brass plaque that was affixed to the white lathing above the garage. A circular wrought iron staircase led up to the entrance.

I knocked and then walked in.

"Well, hello, welcome to our little society." Max was his usual jolly self.

The space was divided into four sections, separated by large wood bookcases brimming with everything from atlases, a set of encyclopedias, books of every shape and size, and a fascinating array of local artifacts. In the center of the room sat a long dark wood table that must serve as host for their monthly meetings.

"I'm afraid that we're out of coffee, but I can offer you a bottled water." Max pulled out a chair for me at the table.

"I'm fine, Max, coffee is not really my thing and it's too early for wine," I joked. "I won't take up much of your time but wondered if you could tell me a bit about the research study you began some years ago on the history of Mar Vista? And also if you intend to continue with the endeavor?"

"Definitely not, that subject has been put to bed and locked away." Max mimed turning a key.

"That is a shame, it sounded so fascinating. And with all the new building and development going on around us, I'm afraid the history of the area could be buried for good."

"I agree, which is why we and this exist." He spread his arms wide to the room. "But I believe that we stopped at the right place in the study."

"Which was where?"

"Just before launching our investigation into the presence of oil in the area both historically and in modern times. It just got too dangerous." Max shook his head in disappointment.

"Dangerous in what way, Max?"

"In every way imaginable. Bad things kept happening, they seemed like coincidences at first, but we realized that they were triggered by our activity in the investigation. I remember being up in the gardens to collect soil samples one day, there'd been a rare heavy rainfall for two days prior, and people had seen small pools of oil in places."

"Wow, what were the test results on the samples?" I could have a baseline here to compare with the sample that I'd given to Frederick.

"That's the thing, before I could get anything to work with, all the irrigation suddenly came on along with the main power hose. The mud quickly turned to slippery sludge, and the water force pushed me all the way down the garden path to the bottom of the hill. I got banged up pretty good."

"Max, I'm so sorry. Something like that would deter anybody. Is anyone else interested in picking up where you left off?"

I heard a thud coming from one of the corners of the office, it sounded like someone had dropped a book. Seeing the frightened look on my face Max explained, "That's Malcolm, come out and say hello to Halsey, son."

It hadn't occurred to me that we had company this whole time. Malcolm had been dead quiet, eavesdropping no doubt.

"Hi." Malcolm showed just his head and neck from behind a bookcase.

"Don't be shy, join us," Max said. "Halsey is asking about the oil research."

He sheepishly walked to the table and remained standing.

"Malcolm was also very interested in the oil portion of this study when he first joined us, so I shared all my notes but watched carefully to make sure that none of the bad omens that had plagued me would continue on with him."

"None did?" I asked.

Malcolm shook his head.

"And has your research been able to add anything to the oil question, Malcolm?" I was excited by the prospect of new news.

"No, not really. I haven't had much time to spend on it, we've been working for over a year now on cataloging all homes within a four-mile radius that were built before 1920. It's an exhaustive process," Malcolm proclaimed.

I'll believe you, Malcolm, just as soon as those pigs go airborne. "Pity, everybody sure seems hell-bent on finding oil."

Malcolm's face paled.

"I've taken up enough of your time, Max. This project sounds like a bear and I'm sure that you both want to get back to it." I rose to leave.

"You mean the 1920s homes?" Max asked, and I nodded while looking at Malcolm.

"We finished that one over three weeks ago, it's at the printer."

"Then congratulations are in order," I said, walking out the door.

We'd never had consecutive Wine Clubs before, but tough times call for desperate measures. We'd gathered at Peggy's and this was billed as a "wear your sweats, we're having pizza and drinking cheap Italian wine" Wine Club.

Of course, with this audience cheap did not equal bad. Since I'd pressed for this meeting, I brought a selection of Puglia Primitivo red wines. They are full-bodied and the notes of dried fruit leather remind me of a Zinfandel.

I recounted my visit to the historical society office in the morning and my conversation with Max. It was a risk and I was hoping that Paula wasn't going to go all cuckoorama on me. When I added that Malcolm was clearly listening in and then seemed totally disinterested in pursuing the study of oil in Mar Vista, both Penelope and Paula gave me their full attention.

"So while Howard and Snyder are still on the radar, Malcolm's behavior slides him up into spot numero uno." Peggy was on her third slice and loving all things Roman.

"He's an interesting fellow," Penelope said. "Did Jack and his dog ever pay him a visit?'

"I don't know," I quietly replied.

In no time they had circled the wagons around me. I'd told Peggy and Sally about the breakup but this was news to the other two. Sad news by their reactions. Paula proceeded to massage all my pulse points, which felt a tad creepy, and Penelope had brought her collection of Cadbury chocolates and wine gums. We all receded to the carpet and gorged on sugar and alcohol.

"What we need," said Sally, lying on her back and staring at the ceiling, "is a clear motive for Malcolm to need to kill Abigail immediately rather than waiting the short amount of time for her to die of natural causes."

"Hmm, what could that be?" Penelope was in the same prone position.

"Let's talk it out, girls. That's the best way to solve this." Peggy had moved back up to the sofa.

"Maybe she had something on Malcolm that he didn't want getting out? Maybe he wasn't a relative after all?" Paula proffered.

"Good thought," I said, "but we do have documents that prove otherwise. And nothing to the contrary has surfaced since her death."

We fell back deep into thought.

"Maybe it's not about Malcolm at all?" Sally suggested.

"Go on . . ." I said, knowing this was going somewhere.

Sally nodded. "What if what she had to tell concerned the deed and the ring?"

"Meaning she knew that they were fakes?" Penelope asked. "I know now that the ring indeed was."

"Let me call Frederick and see if he can now confirm that the deed is also a forgery," I said, reaching for my cell. I went into the kitchen to get better reception. The call went straight to voice mail, and the girls heard me leaving a message.

When I returned, Paula was up and pacing. "It's Malcolm, I know it is. To think that he's been in our home so many times, that he's worked so closely with Max. MAX! I've got to get to him right away and warn him. I've got to go right now!"

She made a hasty retreat out the front door.

"It's not even sunny out," Sally said, shaking her head at Paula's craziness.

"It is all starting to make sense," Peggy said. "If

Abigail had discovered or remembered that these relics were just another scam, the product of her and Malcolm's carnival ancestors, then Malcolm would inherit very little."

"Hence the reason she needed to be quieted," Sally said.

"I would never have guessed that the little red-headed runt had it in him," Penelope said.

"I've been wanting to ask for a while, Penelope, why do you dislike Malcolm so much? We've all seen it." Now was the time, I thought.

"Oh that, well, I don't trust him and I have good reason. I came home late from work one night and wanted to stretch my legs before going to bed, so I took a walk. When I reached his house, I saw that Malcolm was hard at work digging a hole in the soil in a corner of the front lawn. When I asked him what he was doing, he said that his cat had died and he was burying him. I knew that he'd never had a bloody cat. He can barely keep himself fed."

Curious.

Chapter 21

Marisol hopped out of my SUV and marched on ahead of me like she was about to address her troops. In the real world, Marisol was here to collect installment one of my debt to her for saving me from another arrest with the video that showed Snyder bringing the rock to my house.

I must admit though, I would never in a million years have thought that this would be the first thing on her list. I followed her through the doors of the Nails by Magda salon and told the woman at the desk that we both wanted mani/pedis. Marisol was already combing the racks of polish bottles for just the right colors.

I'd chosen a fairly fancy salon. Even though she was acting like she goes all the time, I knew that her nail decorating was done mainly from her back patio. I could always smell the varnish and hear her swearing. Nails by Magda had the most up-to-date chairs complete with six different types of massages, neon lit foot bowls, and all sorts of seat adjustments. Before Marisol got seated, she must have grabbed ten gossip magazines from the drying station.

"You have all those at home," I said to her.

"Maybe, but it's different when you're reading them in here." She handed the nail technician her color choices.

"Those are awfully bright, Marisol, are you sure that this is what you want?" I looked at one of the labels and it read "Jungle Red."

"Of course it is; I can't help it if I'm fashion forward." She'd already cracked her first magazine.

I set up a series of massages on her chair to last a total of twenty minutes. I figured that would keep her occupied and I could relax with my mini spa treatment. I'd splurged and opted for the deluxe package that included a deep moisturizing application, foot massage, and hot stones. The last part was a sore subject and I could have done without it.

There were televisions hanging from the ceiling in the center of the room, allowing for viewing from every angle. The sound was muted but some TVs displayed closed-captioning. None of this mattered to me; I closed my eyes and let the women go to town on my upper and lower extremities. The only sounds I heard were the ambient music and the soft Korean mutterings of the girls to each other. I didn't even stress that they could be ridiculing the deplorable condition of my cuticles. The warm water sent my imagination wandering to a day at the beach with Jack and the dogs.

In my daydream, we were drying off on a blanket

in the sun after about an hour of vigorous paddle boarding. The weather was perfect and we had the beach to ourselves. The sand below had shifted to each side of my body making a cozy cocoon. My head was turned to Jack and his to mine. He was telling me about his desire to learn photography and be able to capture the myriad of expressions he sees daily in dogs and other animals. I told him that I thought that he'd be a master at this because of the way he was able to connect to the dogs' souls. He gave me his most endearing smile that told me how happy he was to have a goal to pursue.

My reverie was interrupted by a low growl coming from inside the salon. I fought not to, but had to open my eyes to see what on earth was going on. When they focused on the room, I noticed that a number of the girls and their customers were laughing. I figured that someone had brought his or her lapdog along. Then I heard the sound again. It seemed to come from the very depths of the emitter's belly and rise up and out. The sound was coming from nearby and the second eruption caused another round of titters. When it roared again, I looked over and saw that it was coming from Marisol, who was fast asleep. Her head had drooped over to one shoulder, the magazine she'd been reading lay open on her lap to a spread claiming that there's proof that Vladimir Putin is the spawn of aliens.

It could have happened.

"Marisol!" I tried not to fill the salon with my

voice. Nothing happened. "Marisol!!" I said louder. Still no response. "Oh my gosh, is that Mario Lopez?"

She bolted upright, sending her magazine into the water-filled foot bowl. People didn't even try to suppress their laughs this time.

"Where is he?" she said, looking around and then up to the TVs.

"You were asleep and snoring very loudly, Marisol. I had to wake you up."

"I was not; you don't know what you're talking about." She was clearly fully awake now.

"Oh, yes I do, Marisol. I don't miss a thing," I boasted.

"Yeah? Then how come you didn't tell me that the developer guy was being arrested?"

I looked up at the TV to see a local news team at the scene of Howard's construction site. He was in handcuffs and a caption was crawling along the bottom of the screen, stating that a large stash of prescription drugs had been found on the premises. I went to reach for my phone to call Sally, but my nails were still being finished. For the next thirty minutes all I could do was watch and it was driving me crazy.

When we pulled into my driveway, we both bolted out of our seats, Marisol went to call Augie and probably check her hidden camera feeds for new espionage. I ran into my house and speed-dialed Sally.

"I hope you've got more info than the little clip I saw on the news," I said before she'd said a word.

"Boy do I, Peggy and I will be right over."

I saw Bardot looking at me expectantly and said, "No, I'll come to you. My girl needs to stretch her four legs and have an olfactory orgy."

They were in Sally's backyard and that killed many birds with one stone because she and Joe also have a pool. I let Bardot loose and she did her rounds of getting love from the humans and then headed for the pool. They have a connecting spa that was heating up for later. When Bardot discovered this, she did what anyone with muscle pain would do: cold, hot, cold, hot. I was glad that she could share in my pampering day.

"It was so sudden and kind of odd," Sally said. "I was closing in on one thousand steps and had just rounded the corner when I saw two squad cars pull up." Sally checked her fitness band to confirm the number. "I noticed Howard's truck at the curb and figured that he was on the lot."

"She had the good sense to call me and I scooted right over," Peggy chimed in.

"Two of the officers checked the perimeter of the lot while the other two went inside the structure, such that it is. You know what people say about places like that? Too poor to paint, too proud to whitewash." Sally then went inside her house.

"We found out later that the fellows were responding to an anonymous tip that they'd gotten, claiming that Howard had been seen selling pills to teenagers," Peggy said, moving magazines and a vase off the low patio table that we were sitting around.

Some sort of ritual was commencing with those two.

Sally returned with a wine bottle in a chilled sleeve and three stem glasses. "I watched them lead Howard out of the fence gate and that's when I saw that he was cuffed. He was claiming no knowledge of any crime and asking for his lawyer."

"I hope he didn't mean Snyder," I said, holding my glass up for Sally to pour.

"I'd joined Sally by then, and we watched the officers put him in the back of one of the cars. I asked and they said that a warrant had been issued to search the entire lot."

Peggy took in a deep noseful of her wine's aroma and then swished a sip around her palate. Her face relaxed into a look of satisfaction.

"It didn't take them long; I guess Howard didn't feel that it was necessary to fully camouflage his narcotics." Sally topped off my wine.

"This is nice, what is it?" I asked, taking a sip.

"It is, isn't it?" Sally said. "I'm not used to drinking a chilled red, but it works perfectly for this Andre Dezat & Fils Sancerre. It brings out the light, floral, dry sweetness. I'm very happy with this discovery, and if the wine merchant hadn't told me how to serve it, we'd never have gotten the full bouquet."

"So where were the drugs when they were found?" I asked; time to get back to business.

"They said that a large bag holding a number of

smaller bags containing the pills was sitting in a toolbox under the top tray. The box was right inside the doorframe under some hooks on a crossbeam where jackets and protective eyewear was hanging." Peggy watched for my reaction.

"I am very familiar with that section of the development, I even have photos of it from when I discovered Snyder's bowler. I don't remember seeing a toolbox. I'm guessing that this would be a large box, several feet long and deep?"

Sally nodded. "I peeked in after they brought the bag out."

I was scrolling through the photos on my phone and found what I was looking for.

"See? Nothing under the coats but dirt." I passed my phone to them.

"This must have been Howard's last Hail Mary effort to get some cash. He probably put it there so that he could quickly make his transactions at the fence. Just like I do with my bucket of candy on Halloween," Peggy said.

"Which reminds me," Sally responded. "I propose that this year we all gather in the driveway of one of our houses and combine all our candy. That way we can be together, drink wine, snack, and not have to keep getting up and down. My knees aren't as young as they look."

"You're always thinking, Sally." Peggy patted her back. "Bravo!"

"I wonder who the anonymous caller was?" I mused. "Maybe Carlos's wife? Did the cops say whether it was a male or female voice?"

"We didn't think to ask," Sally said, dejected.

"I bet Marisol will know. She was calling Augie when I came over here."

"I'm sure that there is a long list of people that Howard owes money to. Anyone who knows what he'd been up to could have called it in. They may be hoping that if he goes to prison the property will be sold and they can recoup some of the money owed." Peggy made a good case that it really could have been anybody.

"I'll let you know what I find out on my end," I said, signaling for Bardot to extricate herself from the spa. She happily marched over to where we were sitting and shook her body, showering us with warm water.

"You're welcome," I said.

Marisol was out when I returned home, so I put on a pot of water for tea and sat down on the sofa to gather my thoughts. I'd really made a fine mess out of my life in the last month or so. Why do I need to always complicate things rather than just going with the flow of it? I'd made so many great new friends, I'd met a man that I loved, I lived in a great neighborhood with my loving dog, and yet I was feeling so alone. Like a single passenger stuck at the airport because her flight was permanently delayed. I jumped when my cell phone went off.

It was Frederick.

"Hello, dear, I'm returning your call and was happy to have an excuse to hear your lovely voice again."

I'll never tire of his pleasantries.

"Thank you, Frederick, I hope you are well. I'd called earlier for one final check on the deed. Can you confirm that it is actually an excellent forgery?"

"And here I'd hoped that you were phoning to arrange another drinking contest. I want you to meet my wife, she's got a hollow leg and will put you to the test."

"I'd like that very much." I laughed. "I am almost in the clear on this Abigail Rose murder and when I am, we will need to celebrate."

"You think that you've got your man, do you?"

"Yes, we all do. Everything points to the great grandson, Malcolm. I'm just tying up loose ends."

"Well, then I won't stand in your way. I can confirm that the deed is indeed a fake. That was another pun, wasn't it?"

"Very good, Frederick. There is one other thing that I was hoping you could help me with."

I explained to him what I needed and he was eagerly onboard.

The tide was way out, and while the early afternoon sun was beating down on the sand, a constant breeze made the air a bit chilly. I sat on a blanket wrapped in an oversized cotton sweater and had protected my face from the elements with a big canvas floppy hat. From behind I could have been anyone.

I watched the sandpipers scatter in the surf and saw the bubbles from shellfish come up through tiny holes in the sand where they were buried. It was another beautiful day in paradise. I heard the panting of a dog approaching and then a soft whistle that I knew would send the dog into a down position.

"Excuse me, are you Frederick's friend, Ann? I'm Jack, the dog trainer. He said your pet was afraid of the waves?"

I turned around and took off my hat. I saw that he had done the same with his baseball cap; Frederick's manners were rubbing off on him. My giant looked handsome and nurturing and it was all I could do not to jump up into his arms. But I had to wait for his reaction.

"Halsey? What are you—Oh, I get it, did Frederick put you up to this?"

"Actually, I was the one who put Frederick in the instigator role. I've missed you, Jack." This time there was no holding back; I pulled him down to the blanket and crawled into his arms.

We both repeatedly said, "I'm sorry" in between kisses and tears.

"This is all my fault, I just can't leave things well enough alone and focus on myself and the people I love. I've always got to be chasing what's over the rainbow. It's not the first time that this Dorothy had to be reminded that there's no place like home." I reached for the wine that I had put in my picnic basket.

"That's just it, Halsey, I don't want you to change. I'm not going to settle for a watered-down version of the girl I fell in love with. I'm the one who has to get better at going with the flow and enjoying when things are unpredictable, even a bit dangerous."

"Sounds like we could both use some training," I said, pulling the cork from the wine bottle.

"I can't believe that you came to the beach without Bardot, if she ever found out, she'd never forgive you."

"Who says that I did? Bardot, come!"

Jack whistled for her.

When she came running, Jack looked at me astonished.

"I'm impressed, how'd you get her to stay quietly on the other side of those rocks?"

Bardot spotted Clarence, Jack's giant schnauzer, and the two raced into the waves.

"It was easy really; I just needed to give her some friends to play with."

"You mean some kids, other dogs."

"There weren't any so I had to improvise. I dug a hole in the sand right by the rocks and filled it with water. Then I dug up some sand crabs and placed them in the hole. Bardot was fascinated and every time one of them would come up out of the sand Bardot would try to play with them. They'd go right back under. I created a doggie version of Whack-A-Mole."

"You're brilliant," he said.

"I love you."

"I love you more."

"Okay, ew, that made my tooth ache," I said, ever the romantic.

Chapter 22

We spent the rest of the week working, eating, sleeping, and mooning over each other. We shared secrets and dreams and pretty much ignored anything going on outside our blissful bubble. But by the following Monday, we both showed signs of needing to "get on with it" as British Penelope would say.

I had the next stage of my website progress to present to the Coast Guard and Jack was starting a three-day intensive training seminar for CARA with the human/canine rescue teams. This time when we parted there was no tension; we'd clearly crossed over into a new area of trust and commitment.

When we both walked out the front door, Marisol naturally was perched on my porch, spying at the neighborhood.

"You have no pride, do you, Marisol?"

"Good morning," Jack said, giving her a peck on the cheek.

"At least one of you has some manners."

"I've got to go, hon, call you later."

We watched Jack board his monster truck and drive off.

"So I see that you two have made up," Marisol said, giving me a very blatant once over. "For the last four days."

"I'm going to create an online data tracking site for you so that you can keep tabs and stay current with all your espionage victims, Marisol." I was smiling though I wasn't going to let anything spoil my mood today.

"Don't need it, I keep everything up here." She pointed her crooked index finger to her head.

"Is that why you forgot to change out of your nightgown? Too many other things crowding your brain?"

"I'm in the middle of handwashing my unmentionables, they're soaking."

"Does that mean that you're not wearing—" I stopped myself and quickly sang a Christmas carol to put the thought out of my mind.

"The redheaded boy is looking for you."

"Malcolm?"

"If that's his name."

"What does he want?"

"How should I know?"

"Seriously?"

After my meeting in the Marina, I decided to be bold and pay a visit to Malcolm. He was looking for me after all. His house was in moderate disrepair on the outside as workmen with three different disciplines were hard at work on renovations. Old broken stucco was being chipped away all the way down to the chicken wire and wooden beams. Electricians were working inside and out; I'd heard that the house came with its original wiring. Since the front door was open, I wandered inside where I saw engineers testing samples in the trench that was to become a basement.

Déjà vu all over again.

I made a beeline away from that and wandered into the other side of the house.

"Malcolm?" I called out although I was kind of hoping that he wasn't home so that I could do some uninterrupted sleuthing.

No response.

It was clear that the dining room hadn't been touched since Abigail had lived here. It was less a dining room and more of a curious antiques collection. I admired an Empire-style mahogany chifforobe that contained table linens, candleholders of all shapes and sizes, and Belgian lace serviettes. Remnants of a finer time. I knew that I was treading on thin ice the longer I stayed here, but these artifacts were just so fascinating. Penelope would have gone crazy if she'd been here.

On a stand in one corner, an antique wooden tommy submachine gun with its distinctive drum magazine stood on display. It looked like it had been taken off a dead gangster in Chicago circa 1920. It was cool but nothing that would help me in this case.

An antique curio cabinet hung on the opposite wall and through the glass panes I could see lots of items that needed exploring. I didn't dare open it, but I found that if I closed the drapes to shield the sun, then I could see clearly through the small windows. A switch I found turned on some doll house lights mounted inside.

Wow. I hoped that Malcolm appreciated what he had here. Or was he just so determined to inherit his oil fortune that he planned to raze all of this to the ground and build one of those Walmart-sized concrete box homes that are appearing all over?

In a plain silver frame was a cover of a magazine called *The Land of Sunshine*. It was dated August 1900 and carried an illustration of a panoramic scene of snow-topped mountains on the horizon line, vast agricultural fields on the left, and majestic palm trees on the right.

On a small easel perched a silver spoon with an illustration of the Auditorium and Ship Hotel in Venice, California etched into the bowl. It was becoming clear that this hanging box held mementos that Abigail Rose treasured since she'd arrived in California. I next studied a brass gondola made to honor Abbot Kinney.

I was about to go until I spotted a ticket stub that was very faded and brittle. Across the top it read: ADMIT ONE—VENICE BEACH'S BEST FREAK SHOW. In the center was a very disturbing sepia photo of a contorted woman in a corset and garter belt. The caption read: "See the strange Z-shaped woman" and that was exactly what her body looked like. Her waist was parallel with the floor and her chest and head sat perfectly vertical.

Across the bottom of the ticket it said: *Oddities and wonders courtesy of the Abernathy Bros.*

"Can I help you, miss?" I heard from behind me and jumped three feet into the air.

I turned and was relieved to see that the voice came from someone in the construction crew rather than from Malcolm. I sure didn't want to be caught snooping red-handed.

I quickly composed myself. "Yes, I'm looking for Malcolm whom I heard was looking for me. We seem to keep missing each other. I called out for him, but with all this noise, I suppose that he didn't hear me." *Was that great or what?* "Is he on the lot somewhere?"

I gave the man my best chest out and smile pose. It seemed to be working.

"No, he is not here right now. Are you his girl-friend?"

"What? No, I'm just a neighbor from up the street."

"You had lunch already? Me and the boys are about to take a break and I know that everybody would be happy if you joined us."

He gets an A for effort.

"Thank you, I have eaten, and I must get back to work." He stepped aside so that I could pass him.

"What kind of work do you do? You need any work done on your house?"

By that point I was out the door and making a hasty retreat to Sally's house.

"That is downright creepy," Sally said after I told her about the curio cabinet.

"Right? Now I'm more convinced than ever that Malcolm killed Abigail. Look at his bloodline; they were a bunch of con artists with a penchant for the macabre."

"It looks like in his family crazy didn't skip a generation. So, Halsey, now that we know that the deed and ring are fakes, giving Malcolm a motive for doing away with his great-grandmother, what's to stop us from going to the police?"

"Nothing, I guess, although the evidence is all circumstantial. What we really need is tangible proof to tie him to the gravesite. To show that he'd been looking for the deed this entire time."

We both sat in silence for a couple of minutes, thinking.

"Wait a minute." Sally sat up straight. "Malcolm doesn't know that these items are fakes, does he?"

"I don't think so. Brilliant! All I have to do is tell him where I've hidden the deed and then walk him up to the gardens. You all could be hiding near my plot and record the entire thing. Then we'd really have something to take to the cops."

"Halsey, I was thinking that we should involve the cops. This guy is a murderer."

"It would take too long to get Augie onboard, Sally. In the meantime he could learn about the fakes somehow, like from his neighbor Paula. No, we've got to do this today. He knows that I am looking to talk to him, that makes things easier."

"Why do I know that you've got a plan?"

"Because we're BFFs. And don't worry, I'll make sure to bring Bardot with me on this mission."

I then outlined what we needed to do.

Chapter 23

With the sting operation set in motion, it dawned on me that in the spirit of our new sharing relationship I'd better tell Jack about the plan.

"Hey, babe," he answered out of breath.

"Hi, I know that you're up to your knees in fur and wagging tails, but I just wanted to give you an update on the Abigail Rose case."

"Okay, your three teams will ride in the helicopter with me to the crash site. Let's get the dogs loaded into the back."

He really was in the midst of a training rescue mission, and I felt guilty for interrupting him.

"I'm sorry, honey, what were you saying?"

"Nothing that can't wait, Jack. I'm going to let you get back to your training. Who knows, maybe someday one of these teams will need to help me out of a jam."

"I'll be the one to rescue you, over and over again. You sure that you're okay?"

"I'm perfectly fine."

"Yes, you are."

We disconnected, and I had the nagging feeling that I was not going to be fine at all.

I figured that Malcolm would first try to find me in my office, so Bardot and I headed back there. I'd made myself a cup of Lady Grey tea with cream and sugar and had a carrot in my pocket for Bardot. I sat in front of my computer and opened iTunes, then scanned my playlists. Today I wanted something soothing (the calm before the storm), so I selected the soundtrack to the movie, *A Room with a View*. It was about a woman coming of age in the Edwardian era in England. She has plans to marry but first travels to Florence, Italy along with her chaperone for a brief sojourn. Naturally, she is charmed by her locale and meets a fellow traveler from England who captures her heart. Together they explore life without the confines of the stern, proper demeanor that is de rigueur for a woman of her standing. She is constantly conflicted about what is right to do versus what she really wants to do. Sound familiar?

The first track is "O Mio Babbino Caro" sung by the great Kiri Te Kanawa. I'm transported every time I listen to it. I took a sip of warm sweet tea and started reviewing my notes from this morning's meeting with the Coast Guard. Then came a knock on my side office door that opened to the street. I shot Sally a quick text and then went to open it. As I expected, Malcolm was waiting on the other side.

"Hi, Malcolm, come in. You remember Bardot, don't you?"

Bardot wagged her tail joyously and blatantly stared at his hair.

"Stop that," I whispered to her.

"Yes, hello, dog."

"What may I get you to drink, coconut water, tea, a glass of wine perhaps?"

"Wine actually, wine would be good." He was so nervous that he kept fidgeting with his hands to hide the shaking.

"Excellent choice, I'll join you. Please sit."

He took a seat along the conference table while I grabbed a Grenache that had already been opened. I took two glasses by the stems with my other hand and joined him at the table.

"I'd heard that you were looking for me," we both said to each other at once.

"What, me? No I haven't." The wine had not yet worked its magic on Malcolm's nerves.

"Really? I'd been told—" I stopped myself, remembering that Marisol had been the source of this apparent lie.

"Anyway it doesn't matter, you're here and I'm grateful for the visit."

During the uncomfortable silence that followed, Bardot snuck around the back of Malcolm's chair and jumped up to sniff his hair.

"Ack!" He screamed.

"Bardot, go to your place!" I angrily pointed toward her dog bed in the corner.

"I'm so sorry, Malcolm, I don't know what's come over her." I whispered the name "Jack" to her, and she immediately lay down.

"There is, was, something I wanted to ask you, Halsey."

I smiled and nodded. I wanted him to feel that he could say anything to me.

"Paula, my neighbor and your friend has told me that you've found some artifacts of importance under the soil of your plot up in the gardens. She said that they look to be from the early 1900s. You must know how much I admire history, especially from around this area. I was hoping that I might have a look. She said something about a deed?"

"She's correct. I did find an official-looking document and an antique signet ring both had been sitting in this cigar box." I picked the box up from my bookshelf and handed it to him. I swear that I saw him salivate.

"La Union cigars, I had a great uncle that used to smoke those things. Not a very pleasant aroma."

Now we were getting somewhere, so I refilled his wine glass.

"Mind if I open this?" He was already in the process of doing so.

"Please."

Malcolm took a deep breath. He lifted the lid and placed it beside the box. Inside were the blue velvet pieces of fabric that had protected its contents.

"There's nothing else in here." He looked at me, white as a sheet. No small feat for a man of his complexion.

"Yes, I know. The ring is out for an appraisal; I need to know its value for insurance purposes."

Actually, the ring had been in my medicine cabinet in the bathroom since Penelope returned it to me. I was trying to figure out what I could put into the locket that could come in handy.

"And the deed?" The blood quickly returned in his face in all its sanguine glory.

"As you know there has been a heightened awareness of the possibility that oil is surging under our very feet. The legend alone has spurred some cottage criminal enterprises." I watched his eyes for any expression change. He took a deep breath and stared directly into my eyes.

"That deed is my birthright. I knew that my great-grandmother possessed it and now it's mine. I need that deed; I've searched all over Abigail's house for it! Now please tell me where it is." There was a sudden desperation in Malcolm's voice that made me turn very serious.

"Calm down, Malcolm, it's in a safe place. What makes you so sure that it is valid, and if so, can be transferred to you?"

"I have no idea whether it's real or not, but I have the resources to find out. Besides the house, which frankly gives me the creeps, the deed is the only thing that I've ever stood to inherit from my family. Back even before my parents died. You have to understand this is the only thing that connects me to some sort of family heritage."

Malcolm heard someone clapping behind him and turned to see Penelope enter the office. I, of course, knew that she was coming.

Safety in numbers.

"That was a very convincing speech, Malcolm, lovely really," she said.

"Look, I don't know why you don't like me, Penelope. I've never done anything to hurt you. But please believe me, I meant everything I just said about my family."

"You don't remember lying to me one night when I caught you digging in your front yard. You said that your cat had died and you were burying it?"

"That was you, Penelope? I have terrible night vision and thought that you were Paula. She was very nosy when I first moved in, always coming over unannounced. I was looking for the deed and didn't want her to know anything about it. I'm sorry."

He did seem contrite and I saw Penelope's face soften.

"Apology accepted," she finally said.

"Malcolm, what is the urgency in finding this document? You must know that it will be held up in court for ages, and even once settled, you shouldn't plan on seeing any money from it for far longer."

He looked at me while preparing his response. It was impossible for me to tell if we were going to hear the truth or if he would play us.

"Being an orphan at such a young age, I naturally wanted to learn as much as I could about my relatives. As soon as I was old enough to go to the library and use their computers, I started to research my genealogy. It was very difficult to build any sort of history, my parents had been hippies, you see. They went off on their own shortly after they married and actually none of my blood relatives had known that I existed."

I looked over in the corner and saw that Bardot

had been making clandestine shimmies closer and closer to us. I gave her a stern look and she smiled back.

"This is fascinating but not all together relevant." Penelope was clearly still not convinced that Malcolm was one of the good guys.

"Ultimately what I discovered was that I came from a long line of scam artists probably going as far back as the carnival amusements at Venice Beach in the 1920s. They continued swindling people for generations all over southern California. I'm sure that there are still some running cons today. I first learned of this by contacting a neighbor of one of my great uncles that was still alive. I ended up paying him back the five hundred dollars that uncle had swindled out of him. This kept happening and I was finally forced to abandon any further study. But a week after I quit, I got a call back from someone I'd left a message with, and that's how I learned about Great-Grandmother Abigail."

"And she told you about the existence of the deed?" We still had basically nothing from him.

"No, not at first, Halsey. Which was fine, I was overjoyed just to meet her. I spent about a week at her house, helping her out with basic things, replacing a washer in the sink faucet, getting the floor heater cleaned and in good working order again. Little things that made her life easier. That was when she asked me to move in with her, into the house that she wanted to pass down to me. I was thrilled. I saw myself listening to her tell family stories for the rest of her days. When I was leaving to go back up north to pack, she told me that my inheritance may include something of enormous value, a deed that could be worth millions. She said that she now trusted me with her secret."

I looked at Penelope, searching her face for any hint of reaction to his story.

"So you left on what date, Malcolm?" Penelope asked.

"Um, I believe that it was October, around the fifteenth or seventeenth. Why do you ask?"

"Because according to the police no one reported seeing your great-grandmother after the tenth of October. Did you fly down from San Francisco?" Penelope was really zeroing in on him.

"No. No, I drove."

"So there really isn't any way to verify that your great-grandmother was alive when you left her house, is there?"

Understanding the gravity of what Penelope had just said, Malcolm let his head drop. I poured him some more wine even though I knew that he was done drinking.

It seemed that I'd been elected good cop in this scenario.

"Malcolm, you seemed to indicate that your fascination with the deed was to have some tangible connection to your heritage. When you learned of its possible significant value, did your opinion change?"

"Yes."

Penelope and I both bolted to attention and looked at him. That was when I saw that Bardot was now sitting dutifully at Malcolm's side, enjoying the gentle petting he was giving her.

Et tu, Bardot?

"You see, this was my chance to restore respect for the family name. I want to atone for every dollar that an Abernathy has conned out of an innocent victim. I still have a lot of names in my database from my earlier research, and I intend to contact each and every one of them and pay them back. And if there is indeed oil under Rose Avenue, then you will all be given your mineral rights."

"That's very noble of you." If it were true, I thought.

I looked out the French doors and saw that the sun had started to set. If we didn't do this now, then we'd be hampered by darkness. I looked at Penelope and she gave me a slight nod.

"Malcolm, I think that it is about time that the deed was returned to its rightful owner. Come along, and I'll take you to it."

Chapter 24

As Penelope and Malcolm walked out of my office, I used the ruse of putting a leash on Bardot to lag behind and text Sally again. I simply wrote:

Gone gardening

I rushed out to catch up with them. We were so close and I didn't want anything to mess this up in the last minute.

Or anyone.

Bardot was pulling on the leash and wagging her tail vigorously, and when I looked out to the group walking in front of us, I now saw that there were three figures. The additional person was wearing her trademark gardening clogs that, for the very first time, were appropriate attire.

"Marisol, why aren't you home watching Mario Lopez?"

"I'm taping it," she replied to me curtly.

I caught up to her and looped my arm through her so that I could slow her walking pace.

"You do anything to ruin our plan and I will report all of your electronic spying to the CIA. And you know that I can."

She harrumphed, but I knew she was taking me seriously. With all her meddling and snooping, Marisol learned a while ago that Peggy had once worked for the CIA. In her eyes that made Peggy the most supreme being. And the only person that she feared.

Once on the top of the hill, I noted that the place was deserted. Which was just the way I wanted it. There were no cars in the lot and the baseball diamond was devoid of players. For a few minutes we all stood looking out at the orange and red horizon line over the ocean. A soft breeze made the rustling of leaves the only soundtrack to this incredible view.

"Do you know why I brought you here, Malcolm?"

"I assume that it has something to do with the deed, but I have no idea what. Paula offered several times to bring me up here to visit Abigail's makeshift grave, but I refused. It is just too gruesome a thought and not the way I want to remember her."

"So you've never been up here before?" Penelope asked.

"I didn't say that, I was here once before." His voice trailed off.

"You came to see the gravesite?" I asked.

"No! I told you, I don't ever want to see it. I was here to observe the houses below for the report I was working on with Max. It would have been a much faster way to catalogue the inventory but I couldn't quite see from back behind the fence to the gardens. So I jumped the fence, I was only going to be there for five or ten minutes."

"But you were caught?" I asked.

"How did you know?"

"I was on the bleachers, watching the game."

"If you knew, why did you ask? You don't suspect me of something?"

Malcolm went person to person staring at us.

"Wait, you think that I had something to do with Abigail's death?"

"You said it, she didn't," Marisol piped up. "I'm feeling good about this guy for the killer, Halsey."

"You really should stop watching TV in the middle of the day, Marisol." I was feeling sick to my stomach. I had one more chance to nail Malcolm and then we were back to square one.

"Malcolm, I buried the deed right back where I found it, in my garden plot," I said, unlocking the gate and letting him pass through. Penelope and Marisol followed him. I turned on my flashlight app.

"This way," I said, struggling with Bardot, who was pulling me in the exact opposite direction.

I walked all the way to the far edge of the garden area, the side that abutted the road leading up the hill. I glanced over at Malcolm, hoping for a reaction. There was none.

"This is my plot, here," I said, pointing to a half-planted area with what looked like carrot greens poking up through the earth. I pulled a small trowel out of my garden bag. This whole exercise was meant to trap Malcolm; I certainly didn't want to destroy anything that the person who owned this plot had planted.

"It's your deed, Malcolm, best start digging," Penelope said, handing the garden tool over to him.

He held it awkwardly not sure what to do next. I saw a brief flash of light emanate from the top of the hill. Thankfully Malcolm was staring at the ground and missed it.

"Where should I start?" he asked, scanning the soil for some visual clue like a big red X.

I pointed to the far corner of the plot that was clear of any plantings. While he got to work on the dry soil, I quickly texted Sally again.

Call off the troops, he's not our guy

I looked at Malcolm, he'd barely made a dent in the soil. His was a body clearly not built for manual labor.

"Here, let me at this," Marisol said, grabbing the trowel and getting to work.

All of this digging got Bardot in the mood and she was working on freeing a carrot from below.

"Bardot! Stop."

I looked at Penelope and she nodded to me.

"Wait, everyone, I've made a terrible mistake. I just realized that I'd dug up the deed a week ago to have a friend and historian examine it."

"What?" Malcolm was crestfallen and rightly so.

"You sure, Halsey? How much wine have you had today?"

"I'm sure, Marisol." The anger in my voice made it sound like Mare-E-sol.

"Crickey, then, let's get out of here. It's cold and dark and cocktail hour!" Penelope marched on up the hill not waiting for the rest of us.

"I'll get the deed to you as soon as possible, Malcolm. But the early report from my friend is that it is a forgery."

"The story of my life." Malcolm sighed.

"Come along, dear boy," Penelope said to him, "you're joining me in cocktails."

That seemed to lift his spirits and whether it was the promise of spending time with pretty Penelope or with a gin and tonic, or both, he raced up the hill to join her.

"Come by for drinks, Halsey," I heard Penelope shout. They'd already made it to the road and were running down the hill.

Kids.

"I'm going to let Bardot run for a bit, Marisol. Maybe you want to go on ahead?"

"Might as well, nothing to see here, never was."

"Which means that there is still a murderer out there, Marisol, so go straight home."

She trotted off.

Now that we were by ourselves, I let Bardot off her leash. This was not allowed in the gardens, but if she could run and get her ya-yas out, then I could relax. I assumed that I might be a fifth wheel at the cocktail party, which was fine. I had been wanting to open the bottle of Flowers Pinot Noir Sea Ridge that I'd found for a special price and couldn't pass up. Now was as good a time as any.

I could hear critters scattering as Bardot put her nose to the ground and followed the trails of delicious bestial scents. Hey, maybe she was even saving some poor, unsuspecting vegetables from being ravaged.

By the time I reached the gate to the gardens, the sun had officially set. The moon was trying to peek out from behind the curtain of marine layer that always presents itself at this time of day. The result of the warm air of the last nine hours meeting the cool evening sea air. I whistled for Bardot.

No response. I tried again.

This time I heard branches and leaves being rustled along with the soft pounding of four spry paws jettisoning her up the hill. When I saw her smiling face, I reached for the lock on the gate and readied her leash clasp.

She reached me, wagged her tail, and thrust her nose back up into the air above her. After a couple of good *snoutfuls,* she tore off in the direction of my actual garden plot.

"Bardot! Come back!" I yelled. I was tired now and really needed to get home to my wine, but she was nowhere in sight.

Crap.

Without her excellent sense of smell, I needed my flashlight app again to guide me along the path. Since I'd really only been to my plot a handful of times, I was pretty much guessing that I was headed in the right direction. That was confirmed when I heard Bardot let out that distinctive high-pitched wail.

"Bardot, I'm coming. Stay where you are."

I recognized the pea stalks and the red watering can I'd passed and knew that my garden was just a few plots beyond it. I held out the light and could just barely see Bardot's outline cloaked in the spreading marine layer fog. She stood frozen in place, emitting a low, guttural sound.

When I reached her, I used the light from my phone to scan the area and I saw that we were not alone.

I couldn't make out if it was a man or a woman crouched down in my garden in the fog, but I was pretty sure that the long, tapered shape that was pointed at me was a rifle.

Chapter 25

"Turn that light off, you'll wake them up!" The gravely words were spat rather than spoken, making the voice difficult to identify.

Just as I did what I'd been told, I saw a flash of red hair in the light.

Malcolm?

"Sit down, we're going to have a little chat."

As I did, I heard a match strike and then smelled the sulfur. The match was then used to light a small candle that was being held upright in the freshly turned soil. It cast just enough light to see the garden but little else. I gave Bardot the hand signal that Jack had taught us and she took off. I was relieved that she was out of harm's way. The plot had freshly planted shoots of various sizes all placed in tidy rows.

Who did this?

As I studied the bed, looking for clues, I saw a hand place the rifle down to the ground. It looked old. When my eyes registered the drum ammo magazine, I realized that it was the tommy gun from Abigail Rose's dining room.

"Malcolm? Why are you doing this? Look, you might as well know the deed to the mineral rights is a fake."

"It is? You mean that they're not going to tear up my beautiful gardens?"

"You're not Malcolm, are you?"

"Of course not!"

The fog was lifting and I couldn't resist, I grabbed my phone and shone the flashlight in the direction where the voice emanated. It wasn't Malcolm after all.

"Paula?"

"What did I tell you about the light; turn that damn thing off!"

She picked up the submachine gun and leveled it at me. I saw that it was loaded, which it hadn't been the first time I'd seen it. I had no idea whether it functioned or not, but I was pretty sure that Paula would try to shoot it.

"Of course, I'm sorry," I said, putting my phone in my pocket. "Sorry little ones," I whispered to the plants, hoping to calm Paula enough to make her feel comfortable putting the gun down.

"Thank you for planting all these lovely vegetables in my garden, Paula. I'm very excited to see what comes up."

"It is not your garden, fool, it's mine!"

"But the girls—"

"Forget the girls; they stole what was rightfully mine. Abigail promised it to me for all the years I took care of her, made her meals with my fresh produce, and watched over her when she got sick."

"This was Abigail's? I never knew that, but Sally did say something about this being a probate sale."

"Another lie! They were all jealous. They couldn't stand the fact that with this plot I'd be the largest shareholder in the co-op and automatically become president!"

"Hmm, you think?"

This was not the Paula I knew. In the moonlight, I could now see her face and her bulging eyes filled with anger. I felt a profound sadness for her.

"Listen, Paula, why don't we get out of the night air and go to my house for a glass of wine? I'll sign the plot papers over to you and this will all be yours to preside over."

"I can't leave my babies now. And I've got to find that deed and destroy it. They can't find oil; that would destroy everything!"

"I can help with that," I said and took my trowel out of my garden bag. With that action, she picked up the gun and touched the end to my forehead. I dropped the shovel and put up my hands. I prayed to myself that the tommy gun was fake and just another Abernathy con.

"I know where I buried the deed, Paula; I was just going to dig it up."

After a moment to think about it, she said, "Go ahead, but know that I'm watching you."

"Oh I know, believe me."

I crawled to the far end of the plot and gently started moving soil. I'd buried the watertight plastic pouch deep enough to be safe from scavenging critters. When I felt that I'd dug deep enough, I put down the trowel and used my hands to feel for the edge of the envelope. I worked with my fingers spread, clearing dirt from the center of the hole to the rims in opposite directions. On my third sweep, I felt the rigid edge of the plastic. I gave it a good tug and it released from the ground. I immediately handed it to Paula.

"It's worthless, I promise you."

"All the same, I don't want anybody getting any smart ideas. That was why I had to stop Max and his damn oil study. That can of worms is not going to be opened again."

Paula opened the pouch and pulled out the document. She spent a minute examining it, the tommy gun resting across her lap. If there was ever a time to make a run for it, this was it. Just as I used my palms to make purchase with the ground to facilitate a leap up, she held the deed over the candle flame. It ignited, causing a burst of bright light that made an escape much more risky.

"What did you mean when you said you had to stop Max with his study?" We were both transfixed on the burning document that started this whole mess.

"Just that, I couldn't have him going around and testing for oil. I had to sabotage the study to protect the gardens."

"So all those bad omens, the dead bird and all, that was you?"

"I'm not proud of it, but dear Max can be very stubborn."

"And what about the power hose that was turned

on here in the gardens? Max had a terrible fall, you could have killed him!"

"I was watching closely, if anything serious had happened to him, I'd have been right there. It did the trick and he stopped doing his research so 'no harm, no foul' as they say."

If she would go to that extreme with her husband to protect her gardens, I felt my spine go cold thinking about what she would do to me.

The deed had burned down to ashes, but the moon in the clear sky now provided enough illumination for me to see Paula clearly. And vice versa.

"I'm just reaching in my pocket for a tissue, Paula," I warned, holding the flap open with one hand while reaching in with the other. I woke my phone up and launched the voice recorder before producing the wipe. I figured that even if she did try to shoot me there'd be some record of what happened for the people who later found me.

"Do you want to talk about Abigail?" I asked her.

"We might as well. She had dementia. It came on slowly for her but then turned much more aggressive during the last two years. The ravages of the disease made her mean, especially to me."

"That's too bad."

"Yes. Abigail was eccentric but I did consider her a friend. She'd always been a loner and rarely talked about herself or her family, but when she got sick, she stopped going out at all. She wanted to die. If I hadn't brought in groceries each week and meals, she certainly would have, right there in the house."

"That must have been very tough on you." I looked up at Paula and saw that she was cradling a small plant shoot that she'd pulled out of the ground. I tried to hide my shock. This showed me just how much of a loose cannon Paula was right now.

"I didn't mind. I love feeding people. It was her sharp words that got to me. She called me the devil, accused me of conjuring up spells against her and Max. She had all that old carnival stuff around her house; I wondered if her brain was going back to the memories of when she was a child in Venice Beach."

Interesting.

"What about when Malcolm appeared on the scene? Did she treat him the same way?"

"Not at all, she thought that he walked on water. That week he stayed with her was like giving her a new lease on life."

So Malcolm is one of the good guys.

"When he was leaving to go and prepare to move in with her, I overheard Abigail tell him about a deed, one that could be worth millions. Well, it had to be for mineral rights, so one night when Max was sleeping, I got down all his documents from the study and searched for clues about this deed."

"Is that when you read the story about the murder of Jeanne French? In the old *Herald-Express*?"

"How did you know about that? I removed those pages."

"Did you kill Abigail Rose, Paula?"

"What? No, of course not. I just helped her pass peacefully."

"By burying her alive?" I shouted.

"She was dead, damn it. I don't care what the autopsy report says."

"Okay, tell me what happened." I shifted so that the pocket with my phone in it was pointed in her direction.

"After Malcolm left she deteriorated badly. I tried to convince her otherwise, but she was certain that he had abandoned her. She started refusing to eat and was withering away to nothing. The most that I could do was get her to take a few sips of the pea soup I'd made her."

"Poor thing."

I watched as Paula gently placed the plant shoot back into the ground and re-covered it with soil. She then dug up one next to it and held it in her arms like a baby.

"A few nights later I was home alone, Max was playing a jazz concert benefit for the museum in Santa Monica. I heard a loud crash coming from next door and I rushed over to check on Abigail. I have her keys so I let myself in. I found her face-down on the rug. She'd knocked over an end table and lamp in her fall. I turned her over, and her frail face was as white as a sheet. I leaned in close to see if she was still breathing."

I rubbed my hands together for warmth. I had the chills not just from the cool night air but also from Paula's harrowing story.

"Abigail was dying. Her gasps for air were shallow and raspy and her eyes were totally unfocused. 'Do you want me to help you cross over?' I asked her. She gave me a nod. I took a throw pillow from the armchair and placed it over her face. She didn't struggle or fight me at all. That's how I knew that I was doing the right thing. I held the pillow until I felt her body go limp. That's when I knew that she was gone."

I let out a deep breath. How tragic, Paula had really thought that she was carrying out a mission of mercy by helping Abigail to die. She was on a Doctor Kevorkian crusade. I looked at her cradling the plant and felt tears starting to well up in my eyes.

"So you brought her body up here?" I finally asked.

"It seemed like the right thing to do. This had been her land and she deserved to return to it. She was such a slight thing by that point that it was easy for me carry her to my car. I always have my wagon and shovels in the trunk, so I had everything I needed to bury her. I figured that she'd be able to decompose undisturbed since the plot was mine now and no one else could touch it. Plus, the compost would enrich the soil beyond belief."

I quickly pulled my hands away from the clump of dirt I had been playing with. While Paula was burying her, she had no idea that Abigail was still alive, just barely.

"Paula, I'm so sorry that you had to go through this. What you did was completely understandable, and I'm fairly certain that anybody would feel the same way."

I had to convince her that I was on her side and that she would not have to face any repercussions from her actions. It was the only way that I was going to get off this hill alive.

"I'm glad that you finally see things my way, Halsey."

"And then I came along and messed everything up. I suppose that you never guessed that the fact that Abigail was declared missing rather than deceased would hold up the execution of the will. That the plot would remain in limbo until things could be sorted out?"

"Exactly and when the annual fee wasn't received the plot became available and the girls swooped in and took it right out of my hands."

"All because of a series of innocent events that amounted to inconvenient timing for you, Paula."

We both stared at each other, trying to figure out what to do next.

"Well, let's go back to Rose Avenue and sort this whole mess out," I said, standing. Paula got up as well, and I felt that this horrible ordeal was finally coming to a close.

"Halsey?" We heard a voice call out in the distance. I looked up to the top of the hill and saw the jerky rays of illumination that meant people were walking while carrying flashlights.

"You tricked me, this was a trap wasn't it, Halsey?" Paula screamed at me and grabbed the rifle from the ground.

"No, I wouldn't do that to you," I said, hoping that those words wouldn't be my last.

"Halsey!" Another shout went out, this one closer to us.

When I turned to look back at Paula, she was gone.

So was the tommy gun.

Chapter 26

"Over here!" I yelled back. "But be careful, best to crawl real low to the ground, she's got a gun. I'll meet you halfway."

The last time my name was called I recognized Sally's voice. I hoped that she had brought along reinforcements. I dropped down to the ground and reached for my phone so I could light the way. When I touched the home button nothing happened, the recording must have sapped the last bit of juice out of the battery.

Inching along mostly by feel, I found a clearing that I prayed was the pathway. It seemed to follow a grid pattern but then again the entire hill was mapped out into rectangles. All of a sudden, I heard the whoosh of leaves and branches and saw something lunge toward me. It flattened me and only when I felt the sloppy wet kisses did I realize that it was Bardot.

"Good girl," I whispered to her, "you went and

got help just like we practiced." I held her close and motioned for her to lie down next to me.

"Halsey, is that you over there?"

"Yes, Sally, but you guys stay down. It's Paula and she's got a gun."

"What in the heck?" Sally said in disbelief.

"I'll be right back, you guys stay where you are." This time it was Marisol's voice that I heard.

"Don't bother coming back unless you've brought the cops with you!" I yelled back.

"Already called them," Marisol retorted.

I saw a light moving in my direction parallel to the ground. When Bardot started wagging her tail, I knew that it was Sally.

"You do get yourself in the oddest of situations, Halsey," she said, reaching me. "Boy howdy."

"Keep your voice down. Paula has Abigail's antique tommy gun and it's loaded."

"That old thing will never work."

I hoped that Sally was correct.

"Paula admitted to killing the poor old lady. She claims that Abigail was moments away from dying and she was just helping her along. I've recorded the entire confession. You can hear it as soon as I charge my phone."

"What? That's an awful slippery slope Paula's on."

"I know, but I believe her when she says that she thought that she was doing the right thing. It should help her case in the long run."

"Paula, walk out to the clearing and give yourself up!" Sally shouted into the air. "We'll help you get a fair and just hearing."

We heard the deafening BRAT-A-TAT! sound of a machine gun piercing the air.

"Bless her heart; she got that thing to work!"

"Sally, we are sitting ducks here. We've got to find our way to safety."

All three of us started shimmying toward the top of the hill. Bardot, thinking that this was some version of the "play dead" game, kept shoving her nose under me, trying to turn me over.

We stopped short when we heard the sounds of music echoing from the hill. It was coming from a saxophone and appeared to be live. After a few bars I recognized the tune, it was one of my favorites, "These Foolish Things."

A car's headlights lit up the access road so that we could see the musician. And that was when I totally lost it.

With tears streaming down my face, I watched Max, pork pie hat and all, serenading his bride. His playing was flawless, and I now understood completely what drew Paula to him on that unseasonably warm day on Venice Beach so many years ago.

Max traversed the top of the hill until he reached about the middle of the gardens and then stopped and played his heart out. Sally and I heard car doors open and then saw Marisol, Augie, and another officer fan out. Bardot gave out a yip and that was enough of a signal to bring Marisol down to us.

"Come on, this way," Marisol said to us, wielding a powerful flashlight.

Where does she get all these gadgets?

"Careful, Marisol, Paula's out there and she's got a gun. Crouch down!" I went to her to make sure that she obeyed.

"Get your hands off of me; we're fine now. All she hears is Max playing that horn."

"How can you be so sure?" I asked Marisol, knowing something was up.

"He told me when I went to get him."

"What made you think to do that, Marisol? That was very clever of you," Sally joined in.

"Don't encourage her, Sally."

"Those two were made for each other. I know, we were in a band together for a little while," Marisol threw out like it was nothing.

I knew I was going to regret asking this. "What kind of band?"

We'd arrived back up at the top of the gardens.

"Jazz of course. Paula played piano and they had a guy on drums."

I took a deep breath. "And what was your role in this group of merrymakers?"

"I was the singer, what'd you think?"

"I don't know how I could have missed the obvious, Marisol, it's been a long night."

I was going to have to work very hard to expunge the image of Marisol in her denim dress and garden clogs hugging a mike while singing "Fever."

We saw lights coming from the far end of the hill. When they got in range of the car's headlights, we could see Augie carrying the tommy gun and then Paula flanked on her other side by an officer. Paula's eyes were locked on Max's.

"This is so sad and so romantic all at the same time," Sally said. "There's a lid out there for every pot."

I watched them embrace and then told Augie that he should take my statement. I was hoping to be able to tell this story in the best light possible for Paula.

"Okay if we do that in the morning, Halsey? I want to personally take Paula to the women's facility and make sure that she gets proper treatment."

"Of course, thank you for doing this, Augie. She's not a bad person, just very confused. She thought that she was doing the right thing."

"I know; I actually had kind of a crush on her when I was a kid and Auntie would let me practice with the band."

"Was there anybody on Rose Avenue who wasn't in this band? Okay, I'll bite, what instrument did you play?"

"Xylophone."

I just shook my head.

"I can drop by your house around ten tomorrow to get that statement."

"Sure. Oh and, Augie, one more thing. What was the name of this band?"

"The Diggers."

Of course.

Augie listened carefully to the entire audio file. Some of it had been difficult to make out because my phone had been in my pocket and when Paula got emotional, her voice went very soft. But I have software for pretty much everything or I can find it, so I'd had the sound enhanced. I'd also converted the file to a written transcript, which took a lot of patience. I will never understand how a computer program hears the word "Abigail" and transcribes it as "albondiga" the Spanish word for "meatball."

"What do you think is going to happen to Paula?" I asked Augie, handing him a thumb drive with all the files on it.

"It is very hard to say. The 'Right to Die' law was passed in California earlier this year, but it doesn't apply in this case. Even if Abigail was begging Paula, it must be administered by a doctor and with medication."

"But this case is hardly black and white, Augie, there must be something that we can do. Paula was being driven crazy with guilt, especially after she learned that she was buried alive," Sally said. She'd been summoned to tell her side of the story as well.

"No doubt, she is clearly suffering from a form of PTSD. She's being treated and will be for quite a while."

"If only she hadn't shot at us with that crazy gun. I know she didn't want to hurt us or she could have killed me at any time up there." I looked at Augie for some sort of answer for how to help her.

"What do you mean? That gun hadn't been fired; did you think that it had, Sally?"

"That old thing would never work, I told Halsey that last night."

"But I—"

I looked from Sally's face to Augie's. They were both waiting for me to say something.

"Sound can be distorted in strange ways when it travels up an embankment, especially at night with the rapidly changing temperatures," Augie explained.

"Sure can," Sally added. "As Edgar Allan Poe said, 'Believe only half of what you see and nothing that you hear.' Or was that Martha Stewart?"

"You both are right, that hill can play funny tricks with your mind at night. I wouldn't be surprised if it was being haunted by the ghosts of dead rancheros from the 1900s."

Sally and Augie nodded in agreement.

"One more thing, Halsey, Paula admitted to being the one that searched your house and put Bardot in the bathroom so that she didn't run out into the street. She said that the door was unlocked, so she went in looking for you. When you weren't home, she couldn't resist searching for the paperwork on Abigail's garden plot. I guess Auntie Marisol interrupted her and she snuck out the back."

What was Marisol doing snooping around my house while I was away?

"I appreciate the info, Augie, and I must remember to thank Marisol personally."

It was going on noon and I was exhausted. Sally however seemed full of energy.

"There seems to be only one thing left to do," Sally declared. I looked at her blankly.

"Bloody Marys at the beach, you betcha."

"Agreed, and then a much needed rest," I said.

Chapter 27

It was another day in paradise and this morning we were all packed into Sally's car and headed up PCH to Malibu. Marisol was riding shotgun, somehow she always manages to score that seat.

I was flanked in the back by Peggy on one side and Penelope on the other. In the far back sat Bardot, breathing warm doggie breath into my ear, and a box of plant shoots from my garden. My cell phone rang.

"Hi, honey," I said to Jack when I saw the caller ID.

"Hey, babe, I wanted to let you know that I'm finished with my training up here. I'm going to shower and I'll meet you there. Sound good?"

"Sounds perfect."

Jack had been doing an early morning rescue drill up in the Santa Monica mountains, so this was perfect timing.

Since the whole sad Paula episode, we'd all kind of retreated into our own lives for a while. Jack and I and the dogs spent a long weekend at Lake Arrowhead, a popular ski resort in the winter and a peaceful escape in the warmer months. We rented a cabin and hiked, cooked out, went fishing, and cuddled by the fire. Bardot befriended a duck that we named Cecil, and for a while it looked like I was going to have another mouth to feed when we got home. But on the day we were to leave Cecil met a PYD (pretty young duck) and they swam off together into the sunset. I returned home rested but not entirely healed. That would take time.

Sally and Joe got the remodeling bug and were busy planning and consulting an architect. The ideas kept evolving and changing, but the main goal was to create a separate space for her cousin Jimmy, who was coming for an extended visit. They were excited to have him joining them as the majority of their relatives resided back East.

Peggy was dating! That was the big news for the beginning of summer. It seems that one of her buddies from the CIA, someone that she had actually gone out with a few times before she met Vern, was now a widower. They got back in touch when Peggy was doing research for me on the case. He lives in San Diego, which according to Peggy, is just far enough away for them to be able to miss each other. And for Peggy to have some Peggy time. When you are in your eighties, you're less inclined to hop in the car at eight at night and drive an hour and a half just to be together. We've met him; you could tell that he was a hottie in his day.

Marisol continues to play hermano grande on Rose Avenue. I think I've finally broken her of the habit of entering my house at will with a carefully staged scenario that Jack and I conjured up. We were outside BBQing one evening with ribs on the grill. The aroma of sizzling pork is usually the Pavlovian stimulus needed to lure her over. When we heard her garden clogs clip-clop up my driveway, Jack and I both took our tops off. As the gate opened, we screamed and grabbed the towel we'd had waiting to cover ourselves, giving the impression that we were both stark naked. She made a hasty retreat and hasn't tried to enter unannounced again. After a brief discussion, we agreed that the idea of grilling naked held no appeal whatsoever.

I looked at her profile staring out the window and I tried to imagine what was going through her head. I suspect that even someone as inventive as J.K. Rowling would have trouble with this exercise.

"Marisol, I keep forgetting to ask you, the day that Paula broke into my house, what caused you to come over and surprise her? Was she making loud noises?"

"No," she said to me, always a font of information.

"So what was it?"

"Cheese."

"Cheese?"

"Yes, I was out of that good kind that you always buy and I wanted to make a sandwich."

"You really have no shame, do you?"

"Why should I, you had a big hunk of that cheese, so I was happy."

I could see the sun reflect off her gold tooth as she looked out the car window and smiled.

"Penelope, what do you know about this property that we are headed to?" Sally asked.

"Well, it's all happened so fast, hasn't it? One minute Malcolm's renovating his great-grand-mum's house and the next he's moved to Malibu. And I believe that I am partly responsible for it."

"So I've heard, but not any details." I wanted to hear the whole serendipitous story.

"You'll recall, Halsey, that we left you in the gardens and Malcolm and I went back to my house for cocktails."

"How I wish I'd gone with you."

"After a couple of G&T's, I'd loosened up a bit and asked if I could see Abigail's house. You know how keen an interest I take in antiques and I'd heard from Paula that the house was packed with them."

"I'll bet; I only saw the tip of the iceberg the day I walked in looking for Malcolm."

"And we're talking real old artifacts," Peggy said, "not mystery clocks and Singer sewing machines."

"Correct," Penelope replied. "There was a box of antique brooches from the 1900s that I could tell were the real deal and a collection of posters and postcards from their original carnival days, all very desirable today. There were loads and loads of memorabilia that I guessed could be appraised at around one hundred thousand, but the mother lode was what we found in her freezer."

"Dear God, now what?" Sally steeled herself.

"Nothing gruesome. It was quite marvelous, really and exquisite. Inside was a large metal box that took up almost the whole compartment. Malcolm and I needed to use hot water to pry it loose from the ice on the floor of the freezer. When we got it out and opened it, we found what must have been more than two hundred antique lighters of all shapes, materials, and sizes. There were Cartiers and Fabergés in gold, jewels, and enamels, DuPonts, Dunhills, even early Zippos. I knew that there was a fortune there."

"Wow, I wonder where they all came from," Peggy said. "I'm guessing that they were stolen, given the family's history."

"That's what Malcolm thinks, which is why he is reticent to sell any of them. So he's just hung on to them and occasionally looks at them guiltily."

"So this property that we're on our way to see, Malcolm hasn't purchased it yet?"

"He has, Sally," Penelope replied, "but it may be some time before he can carry out his plans for it. There are still some parts of Abigail's estate to settle as well."

"I wonder why someone would just steal lighters. I mean a pickpocket would go for the wallet first, right?" Marisol might be onto something.

I took out my iPhone and launched a search. While I was waiting for results, we turned off PCH and headed up hill into the mountains. When my phone pinged, I looked at it to see what had been returned.

"I knew it!" I shouted.

"What?" They all yelled, and Sally slammed on the brakes.

"Oops, sorry for shouting. We have good news

for Malcolm; he's going to be able to break ground right away."

"How so?" Penelope asked.

"I've had a running search going on for Venice Beach in the early 1900s. I thought that I remembered something and I just confirmed it. The Abernathy family owned and operated a roller coaster on the pier at that time. One of the brothers had married Abigail Rose right around the same time."

"And? Out with it, Halsey." Peggy was getting impatient.

"And I bet that's how she wound up with that vast collection of lighters and brooches for that matter. She probably stood under the section of track where the cars were turned almost upside down along with its passengers, shaking anything that was loose out of their pockets."

"Well, that's not stealing, technically." Penelope smiled.

"It certainly isn't," Sally said as we turned into a wooden gate and pathway that led up to a stone house on top. Below were rows and rows of land that looked like they hadn't been cultivated in quite a while. As we pulled up to the doorway, a beacon of red hair appeared from around back. Young Malcolm had shed his worn academic cords and bow tie for jeans and a black T-shirt that actually made him look kind of hip.

"I have the best news," Penelope said, running up and hugging him.

"Love abounds," I said to Peggy, who I swear blushed.

"Okay if I let Bardot run?" I asked Malcolm.

"Silly not to!" He wore a wide grin, clearly he'd liked the news that Penelope had given him. I let Bardot off leash and she went tearing down the hill to search for the Pinot section I suppose.

Jack pulled up in his truck a few moments later and let Clarence join Bardot to sniff grapes.

"Are we going to get the grand tour, Malcolm?" Jack asked, handing him the pallet of small plants from the back of my SUV.

"Of course, there's not much to see right now, but I do have the plans pretty well worked out. I still have so much to learn about wine making and the entire growing process. Penelope and I have been taking some classes and visiting some of the other local vineyards. The owners are incredibly giving with their knowledge and learning from mistakes."

"And Halsey has agreed to help us with her garden plot in town to experiment with varietals of grapes."

"I see this as a win-win proposition." I gave them a contented smile.

There was a large picnic table with benches at the side of the house and we all made our way over to it. Not only to enjoy the view down the valley to the ocean in the distant horizon but also because several bottles and empty wineglasses beckoned.

"Any ideas on a name for this operation?" Peggy asked. It was a funny word for her to use. I pictured her in her spy days naming a mission the Tabula Rasa Project or some such cryptic moniker.

"I have actually," Malcolm replied. "And the sign was just delivered today."

He pointed to a rectangular shape affixed to two large logs with a sheet covering the facing.

"Do we all have wine?" Malcolm asked.

We nodded.

"Then let us toast to the Abigail Rose Winery!"

Perfect.

Chapter 28

I hosted Wine Club a few days later and the ideal temperatures made it an outdoor affair. Bardot used the pool as her stage and performed numerous underwater tricks for the girls.

"This cheese is delicious, Halsey, what is it?" Sally asked.

"It is a Comté; it's kind of like the French cousin to the Swiss Gruyère cheese. I like to eat it with a piece of ripe fig and definitely add a glass of the Ressac Vin de Pays d'Oc Syrah. It's a perfect marriage."

I'd decided to do a French version of my signature "great plate" for them today. It is basically a spread of sweet and savory snacks with an assortment of carbohydrates thrown in for good measure. I was serving pâtés, salume, seasonal fruits both fresh and dried, and five cheeses from mild to stinky and delectable. There were crackers and small slices of toasted bread along with butter and a strong mustard. And three different wines to pair with the food that was selected.

"I've missed you guys so much, and the delicious Wine Clubs," Aimee declared. She'd been MIA for much of the last few months doing double-duty, running her frozen yogurt shop and taking baking classes so that she could soon add to the offerings at Chill Out.

"We're glad to have you back," Penelope said. "She didn't miss much of anything, did she, ladies?"

We all chuckled.

"How's Jack doing, Halsey? I've missed seeing him too."

"He's doing great, Aimee. We should go out to dinner with you and Tom soon. Just don't tell him that you are craving really good Mexican food or you'll end up in Santa Barbara before you know it!"

Bardot was now out of the pool and busying herself with something at the far corner of my yard. I'd seen a raccoon recently, just sitting up high in a tree and staring down at my frustrated dog that just wanted to play.

My cell phone rang.

"Speak of the devil," I said, seeing Jack's ID come up.

"How did you know that we were talking about you?"

"I just assumed that you always talk about me, babe. Hey listen, I'm up at Frederick's and he has some news for you. I'm passing the phone over to him."

"Halsey? How lovely to be with you again even if it is just telephonically."

"Thank you, Frederick, we can FaceTime if you so desire."

The girls, sensing that this call was just chitchat, went back to the business of eating and drinking and gossiping.

"I take terrible pictures, so I'll spare you having to look at my old mug. Listen, I have some potentially good news to share with you. Do you remember that baggie you gave me over coffee with the soil and sludge samples from the construction site?"

"The same bag that got me arrested and put in a holding tank overnight, how could I forget?"

"I've just gotten the test results back, and it shows a 92.5 percent probability that there is oil beneath the land on and around Rose Avenue. How about that?"

For a moment I was numb. The thought of opening this whole oil issue up again made my stomach cramp. I also couldn't bear to think of how everyone would react. It was bad enough when there was no proof.

"That is extremely interesting, Frederick, is 92.5 a high percentage of probability?"

"It's not chicken feed, certainly worth another look."

"Yes, I'm going to need some time to process this, and in the interim, would you please keep this between us?"

"Absolutely, your confidentiality is safe with me until you tell me otherwise."

"Thank you, Frederick."

I ended the call and took a generous sip from my wineglass. I looked over at the girls and they were all having a splendid and relaxed time. While Wine Club may seem on the surface to be about getting a nice buzz and tingling our taste buds, it is much more than that. It has become our support system for getting through both the good and the bad. It is about spending two hours in the sisterhood sanctuary made even better by the elixir from the grape. I would never do anything to put that in jeopardy.

We heard a loud, raspy squeak sound come from the back of the yard. Branches and leaves rustled and I saw dirt come flying back in a spray.

"Bardot, leave him alone and come join the girls."

It took a few moments but she finally retreated from her sentry position and marched over to us. Once she reached the patio, I noticed that she was tracking dark paw prints on the surface. I bent down for a closer look. It was not from dirt or mud, it was more like some kind of viscous liquid.

It couldn't be . . .

What the Rose Avenue
Wine Club Drank

2016   **"Elgin Ridge Chardonnay"** *Elgin, South Africa*

2012   **"Crossbarn by Paul Hobbs Rosé of Pinot Noir"**
Sonoma Coast, California

2013   **"Sea Smoke Botella Pinot Noir"** *Santa Rita Hills, California*

2014   **"Hess Select Chardonnay"** *Monterey, Central Coast, California*

2014   **"King Estate Signature Collection Pinot Gris"**
from Oregon

       "First Class Pinot Noirs" *Aconcagua, Chile*

       "Lillet" *a French aperitif from Podensac, a small village south of Bordeaux, France*

2014   **"Joel Gott Alakai Grenache"** *Monterey County, California*

2015   **"Francis Ford Coppola Sofia Rose"** *Rosé from Monterey, Central Coast, California*

2014   **"Leone de Castris Primitivo di Manduria Villa Santera Primitivo"** *Puglia, Italy*

       "Ressac, Rosé De Syrah" *Vin de Pays d'Oc IPG, France*

What Bardot Drank

2018   **"Chateau Eau de Piscine"** *Mar Vista, California*

A Rose Avenue Guide
to Wine Pairing

A

ANTIPASTO:

What goes best with cured meats, olives, peppers, eggplant, soft cheeses, and artichokes? Besides the obvious Pinot Grigio, try to mix it up a bit with reds and whites. For a red, we ladies like to drink a northern Italian **Barbera**. Great with food in general, a Barbera refreshes the mouth and stimulates the appetite. And more food means more wine, so stock up!

AVOCADO TOAST:

Bring on the **Sauvignon Blanc**. We like to imbibe in the samplings from New Zealand, in particular the tart, crisp Greywacke Wild Sauvignon from Marlborough, New Zealand. First, we love saying the word "greywacke" and the more wine we drink the more we say it. And second for its smooth texture and long, citrus finish.

B

BACON-WRAPPED DATES:

These little sweet-and-salty pork fatty treasures actually originated in Spain, so it makes sense to drink a bottle or three from the same region. We've been known to make fast work of Garnacha reds. Check your local Trader Joe's for Garnachas from Calatayud, Spain. And if you're feeling frisky you might also pair these dates with a dry champagne.

BARBECUE SHRIMP:
We're going **Riesling** here, and not the sweet stuff. We prefer something like a Kendall-Jackson Vintner's Reserve Riesling from Monterey, California. The peach and orange notes give it a yummy finish.

C

CRAB CAKES:
Pinot Blanc is Peggy's go-to wine with this delectable crustacean. She's been known to uncork some bottles of California's Arroyo Grande Valley Tantra for just such an occasion.

D

DIM SUM:
This salty array of bodacious bites needs a fruity wine to balance it out. We're partial to a Don Miguel Gascón **Malbec** from Argentina. Try sum!

DUCK CONFIT ENCHILADAS:
An Oregon **Pinot Noir** will do the trick. Cooper Mountain Vineyards has a nice Willamette Valley selection. The refreshing tartness tastes of raspberry and cherry, a perfect combo with duck. Add mole sauce for the chocolate flavor and you've got all the food groups covered.

G

GUACAMOLE:
Don't you go thumbing your nose at **Rosés!** If Margaritas are not close at hand Sofia by Francis Coppola is the perfect dry, fruity rosé to drink while you dip a chip.

H

HAM AND CHEESE CROQUETTES:
A French Loire Valley **Vouvray** is what's needed here. It takes a boisterous taste to stand up to the perfect marriage of salt and fat.

L

LAMB CHOPS:
Since arguably the best lamb chops come from Australia it stands to reason that they've got a wine that will make them proud. We've enjoyed the Aussie's Caravan **Petite Sirah.**

LOBSTER ROLLS:
Mix claws, knuckles, and tails with mayo and tarragon and serve on a buttered, grilled bun and even battery acid couldn't ruin the experience. But might we suggest an Austrian **Grüner Veltliner** instead? Perhaps a Gobelsburger?

M

MEATBALLS:
Of course the wine pairing all depends on your balls! What? If they are Swedish, then Sally always insists on a silky **Pinot Noir** like California's Cen-

tral Coast Hess Select. If your balls are done Italian style, then you'll need to go to a wine that is made to complement tomato sauce. Look to Tuscany and a smooth and tart **Luiano Chianti Classico.** Any other kinds of balls, you're on your own.

MIDDLE EASTERN APPS:
If your platter is brimming with hummus, tabouli, baba ghanoush, feta cheese, and stuffed grape leaves then you'll need to think pink. With spice you most importantly want something refreshing. Time to call in the **Cava;** we love the fresh exuberance of the Juve Y Camps Pinot Noir Brut Rosé.

N

NUTS:
Peggy's favorite. No Wine Club is complete without a bowl of mixed legumes (peanuts), nuts (hazelnuts, chestnuts), and drupes (almond, walnuts). She's fond of the Ghost Pines **Cabernet Sauvignon** and I love the rich fruit flavor and touch of smoke.

O

OYSTERS:
These briny bi-valve beauties make rare appearances at Wine Club but when the season and price is right, we've been known to aggressively consume them. Fists have never flown but hair pulling may have occurred. We're also known to drain every drop of **Burgundy Chablis.** Our favorite is the Domaine Laroche Saint Martin made from 100 percent Chardonnay grapes.

P

POT STICKERS:

If you're not into Sake, then for heaven's sake, open a few bottles of Pierre Sparr **Gewurztraminer** from Alsace, France. It is bold, fruity, and full bodied, just like Bardot.

PROFITEROLES:

If the occasion calls for these fudge-drizzled puffs of cream, or if it's Tuesday, for example, lean to the **Port** side with something like a Terra d'Or Zinfandel Port. The lush, grapey flavors will make even the laziest chocolate stand up and do the Can-Can.

S

SMOKED SALMON:

Whether served on pumpernickel squares with chopped onion and crème fraîche or wrapped around asparagus, Sally insists that the green, citrus notes of a **Sancerre** such as Domaine Daulny will do the trick.

STILTON CHEESE AND WALNUT CRACKERS:

We're looking for deep flavor here to stand up to the cheese. *Or the cheese stands alone!* We like to splurge on **Vintage Port** but we try to keep it down to a couple of bottles. This aged nectar can get pricey. We've found that Portuguese wines like a Porto Cruz Vintage Port is delicious and will still keep us in shoes and socks.

STRAWBERRY SHORTCAKE:
If you don't already, then you're going to think that we've gone over the bend with this selection. We like to enjoy this spring delectable dessert with Red Wine, specifically a **Beaujolais.** Served chilled!

T

TAPENADE:
Transport yourself to the south of France with this tasty spread of olives, garlic, capers, lemon juice, olive oil, and, don't tell anyone, a couple of those little fishies we call anchovies. For salty food like this you want a wine that has high acidity for balance. We like the Clos Alivu Patrimonio **Rosé** from Corsica.

TRUFFLE FRIES:
If we're having fries we're putting on a dress and we're drinking **champagne!** And don't get us started on the truffle oil. For a light-to-medium body and very aromatic flavors, you can't miss with a NV Moissenet-Bonnard Cremant de Bourgone. Tough to put down.

TUNA TARTARE:
We're going back to Australia for this pairing pick. Aimee is a big fan of Fowles Wine Farm to Table **Pinot Noir** from Victoria. Unfortunately she is not a big fan of tuna tartare so she mostly drinks.

V

VEGGIE PLATTER:
If you've invited a warren of bunnies over for a light snack and a refreshing chaser, you can't go wrong with a **Chenin Blanc,** Sally advises. She likes the California Dry Creek Vineyard Dry Chenin Blanc. "But throw some bacon on that platter," Sally likes to add.

W

WATERMELON AND ARUGULA SALAD:
Whether you add goat cheese or feta to this mixture, you'll want something with a smooth balance of fruity acids to accompany it. Since we didn't pay a lot for the food, we like to splurge on the Blackbird Vineyards Arriviste **Rosé**. Peggy calls it "summer in a bottle."

Acknowledgments

I owe a debt of gratitude to the Mar Vista Historical Society and especially to Glen Howell for his insights and uncanny stories of this most special community that I call home. I also want to thank the people who make Ocean View Farms community garden such a magical place to visit, and, if you're lucky enough, to cultivate in. Great respect also goes out to the Los Angeles Police Department Pacific Division and to Senior Lead Officer Adrian D. Acosta. You hardly batted an eye when I asked you to actually lock me in a holding cell so I could experience the isolation. Thanks also for letting me out!

To my über agents and partners in crime stories, Sharon Belcastro and Ella Marie Shupe, cheers! Same to John Scognamiglio and all the wonderful people at Kensington Publishing. And Bardot? What have I told you about coming into the house with oil on your paws?

Please turn the page for an
exciting sneak peek of the next
Rose Avenue Wine Club mystery

**THE NAME
OF THE
ROSÉ**

Coming soon wherever
print and e-books are sold!

Chapter 1

"I hope that wasn't a plane I heard crashing at the airport," Sally said.

"I heard it too as I went out to water the hibiscus," Aimee agreed, getting teary at the thought.

"Which I'm guessing you did in your baby doll nightie again? You're going to give old Keith across the street a heart attack one of these days." I laughed, knowing I was right.

"We'd have heard something by now if it was serious," Sally concluded. "Cheers!"

Ah, that magic Pavlovian word. At the sound of it, we all hoisted our glasses, looked each other in the eyes, and clinked. Rose Avenue Wine Club had begun.

We were imbibing at my house today, an unusually warm Thursday in February that demanded to be experienced alfresco around my pool. All the usual neighborhood suspects were in attendance: the aforementioned Sally, a statuesque African American woman with the long, elegant hands of a painter and the mouth, at times, of a truck driver. She is my closest Rose Avenue friend. Next up, Aimee, our budding young entrepreneur and owner of the Chill Out frozen yogurt shop. Despite her cold workplace, she is far from being sangfroid; she wears her emotions on her sleeve, jeans, hair, and just about every fiber of her being. Which is what makes her so endearing.

Peggy is pretty much her polar opposite, widowed, in her late eighties but strong-willed and quick-witted. In another century, I'm pretty sure that if you walked past her house she'd be eying you from a porch rocking chair, clutching a shotgun resting across her knees. But she's also the great matriarch of numerous grandbabies, so a hug from her is better than hot chocolate with marshmallows on a cold day. Or a fine Napa Cabernet. Wait, maybe I've gone too far.

We were also honored to welcome Mary Ann to the fermented coterie, she's been a longtime neighbor but a new convert to the club. This may have to do with her decision to cut back on her journalist duties at the *Los Angeles Times* and stop to smell the rosés.

"I'm so used to the planes now that I only hear them if something sounds off, a sputtering engine, or complete silence after takeoff. That noise was neither, so maybe everything's fine," Mary Ann said as I passed around a plate of heirloom radishes lightly coated in French butter and sea salt.

Please allow me to introduce myself. I'm Halsey, and I moved here from New York City after a divorce that should never have been a marriage. But since that was almost three years ago, I am firmly assimilated into life on Rose Avenue in this small Los Angeles beach community. I'd say that having been falsely suspected of committing two murders, being kidnapped, locked up in jail, and left stranded in a fifteen-foot-deep trench counts in the dues paying department.

I make my living writing code and designing websites, and when I started my company during the tech bubble, I would never have imagined that I'd be plying my trade from a suburban house on a Chinese elm-lined street with a converted garage for an office. So it goes. In addition to Wine Club, there's a guy, there's always a guy. Oh, don't misunderstand me, Jack is a great one and we actually met because of the true love of my life, my yellow Lab, Bardot. But let's just say that my prior unfortunate affaire de coeur has left me a tad commitment-phobic.

Just to finish the picture I'm five foot eight, blond—okay, highlighted—and I am thirty-six years old. And my given name is Annie Elizabeth Hall, but for obvious reasons the moniker I answer to is Halsey, a nickname that stuck when I was very young.

My dog is an American Field Lab; she's smaller and much leaner than the English variety and built with a Ferrari engine. She enjoys exercise in all forms, but when she's not saving my life, which she's done several times, her passion is diving. Deep underwater. Like twelve feet down.

When no one had anything further to add about

a possible plane crash, we moved on to more pressing business: drinking wine and catching up on Rose Avenue news.

"How's Jimmy settling in?" I asked Sally. "And how are you and Joe adapting to sharing your pastoral love nest with a relative?"

"Hah! No kin of mine is going to interfere with our horizontal hula. Thank God we put in that second story."

"Sally's cousin just moved here from Chicago," Peggy explained to Mary Ann. "He finally got some sense in him and left the freezing winters for a chilled Margarita instead. Speaking of which, who needs a refill?"

Peggy was up and pouring the Gibbs Obsidian Block Reserve Cab that I'd selected, particularly because of its bacon and black licorice tastes. You could put bacon in an old sneaker stew and I'd ask for seconds.

"We've got to get Jimmy together with Charlie. They already have the love of old planes in common," Sally said, receiving a heavy pour from Peggy.

"Maybe Peggy just wants to keep her new boyfriend to herself. How long has it been since you dated? Are these Castelvetrano olives?" Aimee's food vocabulary was expanding.

"The last man I dated was Vern and I married him when I was twenty-one. Never you mind how long ago that was."

"I'm guessing it was when the best way to start your car was with a whip." That got me a punch in the arm from Peggy.

"Charlie's flying in today. I'll send him your way, Sally, and you can introduce him to Jimmy."

Out of the corner of my eye, I noticed that Bardot, having been unsuccessful in drawing anyone away from their wine to play with her, had started tossing some of her sinkable toys into the pool.

She's got something up her furry sleeve . . .

When you enter my backyard with the pool, you'd think that you've landed in the Laki Lani Resort. It is a small tropical paradise with pink bougainvillea hanging over the water, birds of paradise and all colors of hibiscus lining the perimeter. Tiki masks hang from a covered patio area courtesy of me on a day of particularly enlightened procrastination from work.

I watched Mary Ann dial a number on her cell phone, listen, and then disconnect, shaking her head.

"Something wrong?" Sally asked, launching into caregiver mode. (She's a former nurse.)

"It's probably nothing, but my husband Jeb left the house early this morning and I haven't heard from him since."

"Did you try calling one of his friends from work?" Peggy was now on the case.

"That's the thing, he just retired. And he was a chemist, so he mostly worked alone. These days he's always got some 'secret project' he's involved in. He's possibly been like this all along and I'm just now noticing it because I'm home more." Mary Ann seemed to be trying to convince herself of this.

Aimee's cell phone came to life with a ringtone playing Pharrell's "Happy."

"Hi, honey! It's my boyfriend Tom, he's working in the ER at St. John's Hospital," she stage-whispered to the group. "What? No! Oh my God, is he going to be okay?"

That got our undivided attention.

"Oh dear Lord, we'll be right over." She hung up and took a breath. "That *was* a plane crash you heard," Aimee said to Sally. "And Charlie was flying it; they just brought him into the hospital! He's awake and everything, which Tom says is a good sign," Aimee assured Peggy.

SPLASH!

Bardot, having tried every trick in her playbook to get attention and failing, jumped into the pool with a belly flop that sent an airborne tsunami all over us.

"Halsey? Police." I heard a voice shout from the other side of the driveway gate. "We're coming in."

I watched as our local area detective walked in accompanied by two uniforms.

"Whatever it is this time, Augie, it will have to wait, we need to get to the hospital right away to be with Charlie," I said, noticing that he was carrying a package sealed in a clear plastic evidence bag. Augie and I have a history together—I always seem to find trouble and he always attempts to pin it on me. Somehow it all gets sorted out in the end.

"This package has a Rose Avenue address on it," Augie announced, showing it to the group. "Whose house number is this?"

Peggy shifted his arm to deflect the sun so we could all get a good look.

"That's mine," Sally said. "What'd I get?" she asked elated.

"Is crime so slow that you've taken to helping out the post office, Augie?" I couldn't resist.

"This package was removed from the plane that Charlie was flying when it crashed on the runway," Augie said, ignoring my quip. I noticed that the two cops were now flanking Sally.

Not a good sign.

Bardot, having retrieved her last toy from the pool's bottom, had come up for air. When she saw Augie, someone she inexplicably adores, she raced out of the pool and ran toward him. She then remembered that she needed to shake off the extra water and drenched his trousers.

There's going to be an extra treat in your bowl tonight, honey.

"Somebody get me a towel," Augie commanded. "As I was saying, this package was recovered from a large ice chest that was onboard containing frozen fish. We opened it and found that it had a number of prescription drugs inside that appear to have originated from Mexico."

"I didn't order any medications from Mexico." Sally shook her head in disbelief. "Although I can see why people do, the prices are getting ridiculous. Do you know how much my thyroid pills are? Thankfully I'm on Joe's health plan from the university, which is excellent."

"I didn't know that you had a thyroid problem;

I wonder if I should get mine checked," Aimee mused.

"I heard that eating asparagus was good for that," Mary Ann chimed in.

"I WASN'T FINISHED," Augie yelled.

We stared at him like he'd sprouted horns. Even Bardot was taken aback and chose to watch the proceedings from a safe distance on a chaise lounge.

"When we examined one of the fish, we discovered that heroin had been hidden inside it. A quick look at a few more fish revealed the same thing. We counted two dozen such 'heroin packages' total in the ice chest."

"What kind of fish were they?" I asked out of pure curiosity.

"It doesn't matter," Augie snapped at me. "So, Sally, I have no choice but to take you in for questioning."

"What?" Peggy shouted.

"We've all got to get to the ER. Tom says that Charlie is awake and talking. He'll explain everything." Aimee held up her phone to Augie to somehow indicate proof of Tom's claim.

"Have you already talked to Charlie?" I asked Augie.

"No, he was in the ambulance when we arrived at the airport."

"Don't you think you should?" I could see his wheels turning in his head.

"Alright, we'll go to the hospital. But you need to ride in the car with us so I can keep an eye on you," Augie said, nodding at the cops to escort Sally.

"I knew it." We all looked at Sally and waited for her to say what "it" was.

"Knew what?" We asked in unison.

"With Charlie's accident, Jeb gone missing, and my address on this package. The curse of Rose Avenue is back!"

"Well, that's a relief, I was afraid it was something bad." Everyone looked at me but no one was laughing.